Naomi watched, intr

Detective Ford opened the
leash on the beagle, then g
ground.

"Do I have your permission to check your vehicle and
the contents?"

She nodded, unable to speak beyond the lump in her
throat. She had nothing to hide.

The beagle stopped beside the driver's side rear
fender, barked twice, paused, then barked once more.

Naomi blinked. What did that mean?

An expression clouded the detective's face, and her
pulse quickened. "What's wrong?"

Detective Ford faced her, eyes dark. "My dog just
alerted to the narcotics you hid in your van."

* * *

Mountain Country K-9 Unit

Colorado native **Sharee Stover** lives in the Midwest with her real-life-hero husband, youngest child and her obnoxiously lovable German shepherd. A self-proclaimed word nerd, she loves the power of words to transform, ignite and restore. She writes Christian romantic suspense combining heart-racing, nail-biting suspense and the delight of falling in love all in one. Connect with her at www.shareestover.com.

Books by Sharee Stover

Love Inspired Suspense

Secret Past
Silent Night Suspect
Untraceable Evidence
Grave Christmas Secrets
Cold Case Trail
Tracking Concealed Evidence
Framing the Marshal
Defending the Witness

Mountain Country K-9 Unit

Her Duty Bound Defender

Visit the Author Profile page at LoveInspired.com.

Her Duty Bound Defender

SHAREE STOVER

LOVE INSPIRED SUSPENSE
INSPIRATIONAL ROMANCE

Special thanks and acknowledgment are given to Sharee Stover for her contribution to the Mountain Country K-9 Unit miniseries.

LOVE INSPIRED® SUSPENSE
INSPIRATIONAL ROMANCE

Recycling programs
for this product may
not exist in your area.

ISBN-13: 978-1-335-59804-2

Her Duty Bound Defender

Copyright © 2024 by Harlequin Enterprises ULC

Love Inspired
22 Adelaide St. West, 41st Floor
Toronto, Ontario M5H 4E3, Canada
www.LoveInspired.com

Printed in Lithuania

MIX
Paper | Supporting
responsible forestry
FSC® C021394

For God shall bring every work into judgment,
with every secret thing, whether it be good,
or whether it be evil.
—*Ecclesiastes* 12:14

For all the dedicated law enforcement K-9s
and their handlers. Thank you for your service.

ONE

A tragic murder in a blissful setting.

That's how the Denver media sensationalized Peter Windham's horrifying Valentine's Day murder. An involuntary shiver passed over Naomi Carr-Cavanaugh. Peter Windham and Henry Mulder—both Naomi's high school classmates—died of gunshot wounds. Additionally, the killer left a malicious note stabbed into their chests, claiming they'd gotten what they deserved. Worse, the crimes mimicked the demise of three other Elk Valley High School classmates and fellow Young Ranchers Club members in Wyoming a decade prior. Her gaze remained fixated on Peter's barn, looming ahead in the distance with the gorgeous Colorado landscape for a backdrop. The same place where law enforcement discovered his body two months prior.

Why had the murderer returned now?

Why Peter?

Tears filled Naomi's eyes, blurring her vision.

Unlike her teen crush, Trevor Gage, and his friends, Peter—the quintessential nice guy—was Naomi's friend.

Naomi's connection to all the murder victims and the prank they'd played on her at the YRC dance ten years prior remained one undeniable fact. Memories of the horrible night rushed at her, dragging Naomi back to the painful moment with Trevor and his friends—including Peter.

She shoved the unpleasant thoughts away.

Did Peter move to Colorado intending to flee their hometown and the painful reminders, just as she'd done?

The last rays of the April evening sun prepared to set behind the majestic Colorado mountains bordering the deserted Windham Ranch. The headlights of Naomi's Ford Transit Connect van illuminated her path. She drove slowly, navigating past the outbuilding, stable and farmhouse to the barn doors, where she parked and shut off the engine.

Why am I here? Naomi had no suitable answer for the pestering question. She'd contemplated her motives since the last of her tour bus customers disembarked tonight. As the owner operator of her small business, Friends of Foothills Tours, she provided guided tours to common attractions around Denver and the bordering foothills. This night, she felt compelled to visit Peter's property, and she'd driven straight here.

Again.

Months earlier, just after Valentine's Day, when the news first reported the incident, Naomi made this same trip. Due to the heavy law enforcement personnel presence, she'd known better than to intrude.

But tonight, no other people milled along the property.

No coroner's van drove Peter's body to the morgue.

No crime scene technicians collected evidence.

She released her seat belt and opened her door, then paused. The trills of the birds faded as they nestled in the trees that bordered the pasture—void of the horses Peter loved to train. A swift kick under her ribs gained her attention, and Naomi caressed her swollen belly where her active baby boy moved. "We're here, little man. I might as well look around."

She awkwardly scooted out of the driver's seat, reminded that no movement was easy at the advanced stage of her pregnancy.

Time was running out, though.

Soon she'd be a busy single mommy.

It was now or never.

Her ballet slipper flats crunched softly on the gravel road. Gravity pulled on her aching muscles, and she braced her palms against the small of her back, then leaned to stretch. Sprouts of overgrown grass and weeds peeked sporadically through the ground. A soft breeze fluttered the tendrils of hair that had escaped her French braid, tickling her neck. Goose bumps rose on her bare arms. She reached in and grabbed her favorite blue cardigan from the seat, donning the sweater. Then she withdrew her cell phone from her purse and activated the flashlight app, mentally chastising herself for not bringing a real one. Of course, she reasoned, she'd not anticipated coming to the ranch.

Naomi stood motionless, surrounded by inky darkness, and serenaded by chirruping crickets. With one last glance at her van, she started toward the barn.

Rusty red paint covered the wooden structure and a side door stood ajar. The motion sensor light overhead activated at her approach. Naomi jumped back, startled, and pressed her hand against her racing heart. Grateful for the extra light, she chuckled nervously and surveyed the grounds. Long rows of evergreens bordered the lane where she'd driven. Weeds and tall grass had overgrown the landscape. Shadows stretched out in all directions, bathing everything in an eerie veil, juxtaposing Denver's nighttime ambient glow.

Her legs and back ached from the long day of sitting and driving. A walk would relieve the tension. Besides, since her husband Ted's accidental death six months prior, she had no one to go home to. Not that he'd been around much before the mishap.

Naomi inhaled a fortifying breath, passed the barn and headed for the pasture separated by a split-rail fence. Sweet memories of her high school rodeo performance days trickled into her mind, and she smiled. All of it seemed a lifetime ago.

Naomi faced west, where the last glimpses of the sunset disappeared behind the craggy landscape. She inhaled the fresh air. Away from the busyness of the city, she relished the quiet, though it reminded her of Elk Valley.

Her baby shifted again, refocusing Naomi to her purpose. She turned and walked toward the barn.

A rustling in the foliage behind her had Naomi pivoting. She scanned the row of evergreens bordering the lane, then her gaze roved the prairie.

Was it her imagination or did something move in the distance?

"Hello?" Naomi's voice hitched, revealing her fear.

No response.

This was a huge mistake. She had no right to be on private property.

But there might not be another opportunity.

She approached the barn door, placed her hand on the iron handle and tugged it open. It creaked, though she'd expected nothing less. She stepped over the threshold and entered the darkened space.

Something rushed at her.

Naomi gasped and stumbled back into the opened door as a form whipped into the space between her and the outdoors. Her cell phone light captured the rabbit's white tail as it darted into the pasture.

Naomi's heart thudded so hard against her ribs it vibrated through her body. "Stop it," she admonished before sweeping the light across the vacant barn.

Childhood and teen memories of her friendship with Peter fluttered to mind. They'd had such fun, and Naomi considered him one of her closest friends. They'd lost touch after the night of the semiformal dance, except for a single meeting after she'd left their hometown in Wyoming and moved to Colorado. However, she'd not entertained reviving their friendship. Between the loss of her parents, her husband and now Peter, life was too short to embitter herself by dwelling on thoughts of past hurts.

"If only things had been different." Her words echoed in

the empty barn, where the scent of hay and copper mingled. She proceeded farther inside, hesitating beside a large circular stain marring the hardwood floor.

Realization hit Naomi with the force of a tsunami.

Peter's murder scene.

What was she doing here? Naomi again surveyed the space, unable to shake the strange sensation that someone watched her.

An icy shiver traced down her spine, and the urge to escape the area overwhelmed her.

She spun on her heel, hurrying for the door.

Gravel crunched outside the barn, and she peered out, still hidden behind the open door.

Would she be arrested for trespassing on private property?

Headlights bounced on the single lane, approaching the ranch.

There was no way to escape without being seen.

She glanced over her shoulder again, glimpsing the stained floor, and sucked in a breath.

Terror gripped her heart.

Had Peter's killer returned?

Revenge nursed an insatiable hunger. The saying couldn't be truer as Detective Bennett Ford watched through the binoculars. "Now you're behaving like a serial killer, returning to the scene of the crime—possibly to meet up with your accomplices." The sedan approaching Peter's barn slowed.

He lowered the binoculars. If the situation were different, he might find the petite woman with chestnut brown hair and bright hazel eyes attractive. That part of the case file didn't jive. How had anyone considered her a plain Jane? Regardless, the endless string of boring surveillance days following the Mountain Country K-9 Task Force's number one murder suspect, Naomi Carr-Cavanaugh, had finally paid off.

Bennett exchanged the binoculars for his service weapon

and tactical flashlight, gaining his K-9 partner Spike's attention. "This is it! The truth always comes out."

His beagle's tail thumped the front seat, conveying his readiness to work.

Bennett didn't have the heart to tell his partner that his unprecedented narcotic detection skills—a valuable asset to the MCK9 task force—might not be required on this case. The fifteen-person team headquartered in Wyoming was comprised of skilled law enforcement professionals, including local police, US Marshals, FBI agents, state troopers and sheriff's deputies. However, the task force leader had asked Bennett to trail Naomi because Denver was his hometown. He was very familiar with the city and the surrounding area—including the Windham Ranch location. Plus, Spike's nose could always come in handy for tracking. No matter. They were part of the elite group's unified mission. Specifically, taking down the Rocky Mountain Killer or RMK, who was responsible for the heinous murders of five young men across Rocky Mountain states—Colorado, Montana and Wyoming—spanning ten years with the threat of more to come.

"Sorry, Spike. Wait here," Bennett whispered.

The beagle harrumphed his displeasure and curled up on the seat.

For the first time since trailing Naomi, she'd deviated from her normal, predictable routine. Her daily schedule never strayed. She left her Roxborough apartment at the break of dawn and picked up six to eight tour customers at her small downtown storefront. Then she escorted them all over Denver, ending at Red Rocks Amphitheater, and dropped them off where they'd begun. Naomi drove straight home, turned out the lights early and repeated it the next day. Evidently, she'd planned to work right up to the baby's birth. If Bennett didn't know otherwise, he'd assume Naomi used boredom as her weapon of choice. He snorted at his sarcastic thought.

Tonight, she'd finally provided a twist from her norm by

driving south of Denver to the Windham Ranch in Ridge. No doubt, to relish in her latest crime and, Bennett also hoped, to retrieve the 9 mm pistol used in all the murders. The weapon—which the authorities had yet to find—would give him the coup de grâce when he closed the RMK case.

The unexpected arrival of the second vehicle, however, provided the ultimate icing on the investigation cake. It explained how a woman in her final pregnancy trimester killed two grown men in different states—Peter Windham in Colorado and Henry Mulder in Montana. Additionally, the accomplices expounded on Naomi's dire financial straits. She'd paid hired assassins to exact her revenge on the ones who humiliated her ten years prior.

The updated case file now shared the undeniably sad story of golden-boy Trevor Gage inviting Naomi to the YRC semiformal dance as a prank. When she arrived, all Trevor's friends, except Peter, had laughed at her. Now, five of those young men were dead. Peter was the one anomaly, as he hadn't participated in humiliating Naomi. The prank revealed Trevor had only asked her out as a joke. Devastated, she'd bolted from the dance in tears. A month later, on Valentine's Day, authorities discovered three of the teens murdered in an Elk Valley barn. The start of Naomi's reign of terror.

Not that Bennett condoned the young men's unacceptable bullying behavior. What they'd done to her was beyond cruel, and someone should've held them accountable. Naomi's illegal vigilante actions solidified her motive and thwarted any hope of the young men's recompense. In an ironic twist, it turned the tables, offering those same instigators warranted justice.

Peter's friendship with Naomi didn't fit with the other victims' intentions. Though the MCK9 team argued a better friend would've protected her from the start.

Peter's adult life included a spotless reputation. He was an active churchgoer and well-respected horse trainer. Why kill him on the ten-year anniversary of the first three murders?

Unless the death of Naomi's husband and her pregnancy triggered the killer inside? Were they the catalyst for her latest acts of revenge? She'd moved to Denver shortly after Peter Windham did. Stalking him, perhaps? Assuming she'd be far from her hometown of Elk Valley, Wyoming, and no one would piece the cold case murders together?

Bennett's experience with liars, both professionally and personally, had taught him outward appearances didn't reveal a person's real underlying motives. He'd never again underestimate the mind of a criminal, thanks to Delaney Huxley—con woman, drug dealer extraordinaire and Bennett's ex-fiancée.

Everything pointed to Naomi, and she might've gotten away undetected with the prior victims' cases going cold. But she had to satisfy her insatiable appetite for revenge by killing Peter and Henry. Both were found bearing the same fatal gunshot wounds and vicious notes stabbed into their chests with a knife. *They got what they deserved. More to come across the Rockies. And I'm saving the best for last.*

This time, Naomi wouldn't get away with murder. She'd pay for the five innocent lives she'd taken. Women serial killers were less common than their male counterparts, but were certainly not unheard of. Although, in Naomi's case, if they added in her deceased husband who "accidentally" fell off a cliff hiking six months prior, the body count rose to six. Bennett scrutinized that a smarter killer would've purchased life insurance on the victim before shoving him to his death. However, if Ted Cavanaugh had discovered his wife's murderous secrets, that was motive enough for her to eliminate him.

Bennett closed his truck door and crept through the brush toward the barn. He kept to the shadows, then hid behind Naomi's small bright turquoise transit van with massive daisies painted in primary colors, covering the vehicle's exterior. Magnetic signs in a shade of purple Bennett's grandmother called wisteria advertised *Friends of Foothills Tours* in flowery lettering, with several catchy hashtags and contact information.

After spending days surveilling her vehicle, he'd see daisies in his dreams for months after he closed the case.

Bennett double-checked the magazine in his gun. Arresting Naomi as the Rocky Mountain Killer and her accomplices would propel his career to new levels. Not that he'd minded his past service with the Denver Police Department Narcotics Unit, but his position with the MCK9 task force was a step up. After his ex-fiancée's betrayal, Bennett was ready for more than chasing down local drug dealers like Roderick Jones. The criminal he'd started his narcotics career pursuing. Jones had eluded police at every turn. Now Bennett wanted more.

Contentious voices rose, growing louder.

Bennett scurried for the cover of a massive lilac bush and ducked down. Two large men, one wielding a gun and both wearing ski masks over their faces, walked behind Naomi.

Why would her accomplices hide their identities?

Something wasn't right.

Bennett dropped low, remaining out of sight.

"Don't move!" one of the guys shouted at her. "Turn around."

Naomi slowly faced the men, giving Bennett a perfect visual of the fear etched in her expression.

"Stop playing games!" the gun-wielding man hollered. "Where is it?"

"I… I don't know what you mean," she stammered, her eyes widened to the size of dinner plates. She kept her arms low, covering her pregnant belly.

By the sounds of it, her accomplices' arrival was unfriendly. She'd apparently made enemies in her revenge pursuit. No honor among criminals and all that. A twinge of conscience interfered with Bennett's judgmental thoughts. Still, he couldn't help but pity her unborn baby.

The two hoodlums threatening Naomi might buy her innocent act, but Bennett's skepticism argued otherwise. What was the *it* they wanted? Money? Drugs? Guns? He needed more information. Balance and timing were imperative. Closing in too soon risked stifling the creeps from unknowingly handing him the evidence to arrest the trio. Not moving fast enough could cost Naomi her life. Bennett refused to allow that to happen.

The other man stalked closer to Naomi, cracking his knuckles in an intimidation stance.

She backed up, cowering. She must be unarmed, or she'd surely brandish her weapon.

Bennett ground his teeth. Indignation at the ignorant brute's tactics overrode his curiosity at the situation. He would not tolerate watching two idiots hurt a woman.

Even if she was a killer.

But from his position, he wouldn't be able to get a clean shot without endangering Naomi.

"You're going to give it to us one way or the other," the gun-wielding man said.

"Please, you have me confused with someone else," Naomi pleaded.

"Where. Is. It?" he insisted in staccato grunts.

"I don't know what you're talking about!" Naomi cried.

Bennett trained his sights on the gun-wielding man while maintaining visual on the other. They stood too far apart for him to take them both out in a single shot. He had to make it count.

The other shifted as though uncomfortable with the action. "Maybe she doesn't know."

That surprised Bennett. *Hmm.* Unless he was trying to gain Naomi's trust. The tactic wasn't unheard of. Bad cop, good cop, or in this case, bad criminal, worse criminal.

"I promise I don't know what you're talking about," she said.

The man lifted his weapon.

Naomi shrieked and squatted.

Bennett moved forward.

Several consecutive blasts echoed across the open land as the man shot out the tour van's back window and rear tires. A flock of birds nesting in the tree above Bennett burst into flight, startling him.

"No!" Naomi screamed, ducking her head. "I'm nine months pregnant. If I knew, I'd give you whatever you want. Don't hurt me. For my baby's sake."

Her sincere concern for her unborn baby triggered Bennett's instincts. She truly either didn't know what the man wanted or couldn't tell him.

The situation had gotten out of control too fast. "Police!" Bennett bolted from the tree line. "Put down your weapon!"

The men spun in a synchronized effort, facing Bennett, and the first fired at him.

Bennett dodged to the right, avoiding the hit, which spewed bark near his head. He rolled behind a large bramble and returned fire. The shooter's accomplice bellowed, indicating Bennett's bullet found its mark, though he couldn't be certain in the dark. The two ducked into the shadows between the barn and stable, disappearing from sight.

Bennett's gaze bounced between the fleeing men and Naomi—who was still his chief priority as the murder mastermind. She got to her feet and hurried off in the opposite direction.

Catching her and getting her to safety overrode the need to chase down her accomplices. The sound of an engine roared from behind Bennett as the men sped from the property.

"Stop!" Bennett sprinted after Naomi. "Police!"

TWO

Naomi glanced over her shoulder. The stranger with a gun was getting closer. He claimed to be the police, but she couldn't believe anything after what had just happened.

She tried to increase her pace, but her body refused to co-operate.

He would catch her.

No. No. Her feet were heavy, sluggish, as though she moved through quicksand. She pushed through the trees, branches slapping at her face. Searching for a place to hide, she stepped over a log and her ankle twisted on the uneven ground, causing Naomi to stumble.

Like a bird taking flight, her widespread arms grasped for something to stop her fall and she landed hard against a prickly tree trunk. Her cheek scraped the rough bark, and she pushed back, attempting to right herself. Her breaths came out in short pants, and she visually sought her pursuer.

Where had he gone?

A glimmer ahead caught her attention, and she bolted forward. Drawing nearer, she spotted a Silverado, and she prayed the keys were inside.

Naomi hurried as fast as her feet and current state allowed. She reached the driver's side door and turned to see the man appear from the foliage.

"Stop! Police!"

Naomi slowed to catch her breath, though her mind screamed

to keep moving. Regardless, her body was done. Unable to take another step, she leaned against the vehicle.

"Naomi! Don't move!" The man was at her side within seconds. "Why did you run?"

Her eyes roved from his hand to his face. "Because. You. Have a gun," she panted, then blinked. "How do you know my name?"

"I'm a cop," he said, still holding the pistol. He didn't elaborate on his comment, as though his title explained everything. "Don't move."

"Couldn't…if I…wanted," she replied.

He lowered the weapon but didn't put it away. With his other hand, he reached into his shirt neckline and withdrew a chain holding a leather pouch with a shiny badge. "Aside from being on the task force, I'm with the Denver Police Department. Detective Bennett Ford." He stepped back, and a sharp bark from inside the pickup startled Naomi. "Are you okay?"

She turned, coming face-to-face with the narrow snout and wide eyes of a small dog peering out from the driver's side window.

"That's Spike, my K-9," the detective explained. She looked up at a tall man with short blond hair. His brown eyes were unreadable.

"Yes." She took a deep breath. "Just a little shook up."

"Understandably so. Who were those men?"

"I have no idea." She shrugged. "Are they gone?"

He seemed to study her. "Yes, but who knows for how long. Before I put you into my truck, I need to make sure Spike and I aren't in any danger of you riding with us. Are you armed?"

"Of course not." She tugged the edges of her pale blue cardigan around her belly.

"I have to pat you down—for your safety and mine."

"What?" She narrowed her eyes, then gestured wide with her arms. "Is that really necessary?" As though she could hide anything under her long tunic, sweater, and leggings.

"Yes, ma'am, it's protocol."

"Fine," she exhaled.

"You're not carrying any bazookas or flame throwers, are you?"

Despite the seriousness, a grin tugged at Naomi's lips at the silly question. "No, sir, just a baby boy. But he's also unarmed."

"Good. Please lift your hands above your head."

"I understand." Naomi complied, assuming the position she'd seen on TV. For a moment, she contemplated if that was a mistake. Would he assume she was familiar with the arrest process?

He respectfully patted her down and seemed satisfied she was unarmed. "Okay, let me help you up into the truck, and we'll drive over to check on your van."

Relieved he'd not associated her as one of the criminals, she said, "Thank you for saving my life, by the way."

"Glad I could help." He nodded curtly while offering a tight grin. "If those men return, we're exposed out here in the open."

Naomi hesitated, then inhaled deeply, finally catching her breath. "This doesn't look like a cop vehicle."

The pathetic argument provided her the opportunity to stall. What if he wasn't who he claimed to be? In a side glance, she spotted the badge still hanging around his neck.

"It's my personal truck. Hard to do surveillance in a patrol vehicle." He held out a key fob and pressed a button. Headlights beamed through the brush.

In the light, Naomi studied him. Tall, handsome, dressed in jeans, running shoes, and a long-sleeved T-shirt. Yet suspicion hovered in her mind. Except for the badge and gun, not much about Detective Ford appeared cop-like. She hesitated, determined to gather more information. "Wait, you said Denver PD? Why are you here?"

"That's what I'm hoping to talk to you about." He spoke calmly in a matter-of-fact manner.

"You're a little out of your jurisdiction," Naomi countered.

"Actually, I'm not." He stood, arms crossed, and she didn't miss the way his pose accentuated his biceps. "I'm a member of the Mountain Country K-9 Task Force."

Naomi tilted her head. "And what's that?"

"MCK9 is a special task force with a mission to take down the Rocky Mountain Killer, who has claimed the lives of innocent men from Elk Valley." He spoke the words as though throwing down a gauntlet.

The effect worked, and she gasped. "Elk Valley?"

A glimmer in his eyes indicated his satisfaction, and she instantly regretted her reaction. "Familiar with the area?"

"Yes. I grew up there." A wave of nausea swirled in her stomach, and she swallowed hard. Desperate to steady herself and the ground spinning beneath her, she reached for the pickup.

"You look a little green. Let me help you."

She acquiesced, and he led her to the passenger side. The dog barked again, and she hesitated, unsure what to expect. Would an attack K-9 come lunging at her? Didn't cops have those German shepherds or Malinois-type dogs?

"First, I have to relocate Spike."

She stepped aside while he opened the passenger door. He turned, holding a beagle, who watched her with a curious expression. Totally not what she'd expected. "Aw, he's cute."

"He thinks so," the detective chuckled. "Spike, kennel."

Without hesitation, the beagle hopped into the steel kennel positioned in the back seat. Detective Ford offered his hand to help Naomi into the truck, then closed the door.

At least he hadn't handcuffed her.

He slid behind the wheel seconds later, speed-cleaning the set of folders and takeout bags on the floor. "Mind if I ask a few questions before I drive you to your van?" Detective Ford started the engine.

"First, I need more information. Like why you were here to begin with?" She glanced from him to the windshield, wondering how long he'd been there. "Were you watching me?"

"Yes." His answer came without hesitation or resignation. "It's a good thing I was here, or that incident might've had a much different ending."

"True." She couldn't argue with that logic. "Detective Ford, what's going on? Am I in trouble? I apologize for trespassing on private property. I came out of the barn when I heard the vehicle approaching. If they were family members of Peter—" *or the killer returning* "—I didn't want them assuming I was stealing or bothering anything." Aware of her rambling, Naomi searched for a justifiable reason to visit a murder scene. Although, learning the detective watched her explained the strange sensation she'd had earlier. Her mother always said, *Trust your instincts.*

"Those men are determined to get something from you," the detective said, refocusing her attention.

"I don't know what they wanted or what they were even talking about."

He quirked a disbelieving brow. "Let's start with why you're here?" He met her gaze, unrelenting.

Her neck warmed with embarrassment. "It's complicated."

"This is an active murder scene. Not exactly a tourist attraction. But then you're aware of that, right, Naomi?"

"You still haven't answered how you know my name."

He didn't respond.

Naomi surmised he'd ran her license plate, confirming the van was registered to her. A small measure of relief reassured her. "I assumed law enforcement had cleared the area since the yellow tape wasn't on anything. I apologize. I meant no harm." Naomi's ears warmed with embarrassment. "Is that why you're here?"

His expression remained stoic.

"Oh, wait." Naomi's hand flew to her mouth, and she whispered, "Are you watching to see if the murderer returns?"

"Something like that."

She nodded.

"Let's head to your van." He drove out from the tree cover and approached the main road, then turned onto the Windham property.

"Do you think those men killed Peter?"

"I'm not sure." He shrugged. "What can you tell me about them?"

"Nothing." Naomi shifted in the seat, eager to go home and forget the terror of the night's events.

"Did you notify anyone you'd be here?"

Sadness swooped down on her. Who cared where Naomi went any day? "No, sir. No one else was aware I was coming here. Until I started heading home tonight, I didn't even know."

"It appeared like a last-minute move."

His words landed in her mind, slowly taking root, and she gaped at him. "How long have you followed me?"

"It's my job."

"How did I become your job?"

"Answer my questions first, and we can talk about the rest."

What a frustrating man! "I came here because Peter Windham was an old friend of mine, though we'd fallen out of touch over the years. Today, one of my tourist customers talked about how short life is, and I immediately thought of him."

"Are you having regrets?" He turned onto the lane leading to her van.

"No, not really." She glanced down at her hands. "I wish things had been different between us, though."

Why was he asking so many questions?

"Any idea why someone would hurt Peter?"

"No. He was a good guy. Peter always understood me," Naomi continued. "When I moved out here, Peter visited me, but I made it clear I wasn't interested in any reunions. I distanced myself from Elk Valley for a reason." She paused, pondering. "That was the great thing about Peter. He didn't press me or get offended. My husband was all I needed."

"My uncle says we all have enemies, and they're usually those closest to us."

Naomi shrugged. "I suppose."

"Did Peter have enemies?"

"I couldn't tell you."

"I disagree." He pulled up next to her van, shifted into Park, then pierced her with a stare. "Tell me what happened. Did he say something to remind you of that horrible prank at the Young Ranchers Club dance ten years ago? If so, I understand why you did it."

"What are you saying?" Her brows knit together as she processed the information. "Are you implying I'm a suspect?"

"Should I be?"

"Of course not!"

"Aren't you tired of carrying all that weight? Talking to me is the only way I can help you."

"Help me what?" She leaned into the seat, pulse racing.

"Understand why you returned to the scene of the crime. Your crime."

"What?" Naomi blinked. "No. Peter was my friend. I was thinking about him and just came to…to… I can't explain why I'm here. I made a mistake."

"Let's end this game. Why did you kill him?" His question alluded to the confidence of already knowing the answer.

If not for the pain radiating up her back, Naomi might not have had the courage to snap at the detective, but her patience waned. "That's ludicrous!"

"Okay. Tell you what. Let's get out of here and see what damage they did."

Was he baiting her? She reached for the door handle. "Fine."

"Spike's been cooped up in here for a while. Mind if he takes a quick break with us?"

Whatever hurried this along. "Not at all." She climbed out before he reconsidered and continued interrogating her.

Detective Ford walked around the hood, approaching on

her side. He opened the back door, snapped on a leash for the beagle, and then gently placed the dog on the ground. He left the engine running, headlights illuminating the area. "How about it, Spike? Ready for cookies?"

The beagle barked and wagged his tail.

Naomi watched the team, intrigued.

With a flashlight in hand, the detective and his dog surveyed the van's perimeter, inspecting the damage. Naomi trailed them. The beagle roamed to the full extent of his leash, sniffing the vehicle. Naomi paused at the rear of the van, gaping at the flat tires and shattered windows. What a disaster!

"This will cost me a fortune to fix." She groaned, fighting back tears. "Not to mention, what do I drive in the meantime?"

"I'll call a tow truck and have it transferred to a repair shop." He watched his dog. "Do I have your permission to check your vehicle and the contents?"

His words traveled to her as though she were underwater, filtered and thick. She nodded, unable to speak beyond the lump in her throat. Besides, she had nothing to hide.

Spike turned, aiming for the rear tires.

"Where's he going?"

"Good question. Maybe looking for cookies." Bennett chuckled.

The beagle stopped next to the driver's side rear fender, barked twice, paused, and then barked once more.

Naomi blinked. What did that mean?

An expression clouded the detective's face, and her pulse quickened. "What's wrong?"

Detective Ford faced her, eyes dark. "My dog just alerted to the narcotics you hid in your van."

Bennett laser-focused on Naomi. She'd almost convinced him with her innocent act. The idea that the van held drugs seemed far-fetched at first, but his skepticism had won again. He'd surreptitiously instructed Spike to search for drugs, using the keyword *cookie* in their conversation. When he recognized his dog's heightened sniffer action near the van, Bennett was thrilled.

"You might've fooled me, but you won't fool him." He gestured toward Spike, who sat, tail wagging, anticipating his reward. "Good job." Bennett reached into his back pocket and withdrew the stuffed taco dog toy, tossing it to the beagle. Spike snatched it in midair, chomping gratefully.

"I'm telling you, I don't have any drugs," Naomi insisted. "You've checked me. Look through my purse in the van! You won't find anything!"

"Spike says otherwise."

"Well, no offense to your dog, but he's wrong."

"Negative." Bennett snorted. "Spike is never wrong. Let's start at the beginning. Are the narcotics what those thugs were after? Is that how you paid them to kill Peter?"

"What? No!" Naomi shook her head. "For the last time, I don't have any drugs on me. I'm not using them. I'm pregnant."

"I've seen too many drug-addicted mothers-to-be. Pregnancy doesn't exclude you. What are you dealing? Pills? Marijuana?"

"I don't know how else to say this. I'm not doing anything!" Naomi placed a hand against her back. She looked exhausted and worn out, but Bennett couldn't let her go now.

"Naomi, I am a narcotics detective, and my K-9 has the best certified nose in Denver. He alerted for a reason."

She spun on her heel, teetering a little off-balance.

"Careful." Bennett reached out a hand to steady her.

She glared at him as though she intended to refuse his help, but her skin had blanched, and she clung to his arm. He'd seen people faint when Spike found their drugs. The blood rushing through their system and the need to lie sometimes turned their legs into noodles.

"Now you'll accuse me of being high," she snapped. "But

for your information, I didn't eat much today, so I'm sure it's just low blood sugar."

That might be true. She'd not stopped to have lunch in between tours. "Let's have you sit here while we figure this out." He helped her to a crate near the stable door. Bennett gazed at her tour bus. "Spike and I are going to search inside your van."

"I didn't agree to a second search."

"Don't need it. Once he's alerted I have probable cause."

Naomi sighed, saying nothing more.

"Please remain here until we're finished," Bennett instructed, keeping her in his visual but at a close enough proximity should she try to escape. "Normally, I'd handcuff you. I'm going to trust you'll stay there. Don't push me by doing something foolish."

She harrumphed, crossing her arms over her chest.

Bennett and Spike entered the van, and he spotted her purse on the passenger seat. He searched the bag, finding her wallet, two ten-dollar bills, a tube of lip balm, tissues and a package of peanut butter crackers. It was a long shot that she'd keep the 9 mm murder weapon linked to all the cases there, but hope reigned eternal.

Bennett knelt beside Spike. "I need your taco, buddy." The dog dropped the soggy toy to the ground. Bennett spoke in an excited tone. "Time to work! Find the cookies."

The beagle barked and wagged his tail.

"Okay, find the cookies!"

Spike sniffed the interior and alerted again by the rear fender.

Confirmation of the first signal.

He exited the van, meeting Naomi's curious gaze, then ordered Spike, "Stay. Guard."

The beagle took his position facing Naomi. He wasn't an apprehension or a guard dog, but she didn't know that.

Bennett rushed to his truck, withdrew a pair of latex gloves and donned them, then returned to the van. Lying face up, he examined the underside, sweeping his flashlight beam. He probed around the fender liner of the rear driver's side wheel and knocked. The resounding thud signified the normally empty space held something solid inside. Bennett felt around the undercarriage and liner until he located a small door. He lifted the well-disguised latch and found a hidden compartment. Adjusting the light, he inched closer and smiled at the box shape masquerading as part of the van's understructure. He'd seen a lot of narcotic hiding places in his enforcement years, but this was elaborate.

Bennett inserted his hand into the fender well and withdrew two thick plastic bags. He scooted out from the vehicle and got to his feet, holding the object in his hands.

Naomi's mouth formed a perfect O, vehemently shaking her head as though that nullified his find. Satisfied, Bennett strode toward her, determined and angry. He'd almost bought her lies! He held up the bags. "Care to explain? This time, try the truth."

"I can't. That's not mine. I never put anything there."

Bennett illuminated the bags with his flashlight. Both contained a white crystal-like substance that he recognized as fentanyl. Likely illicitly manufactured and deadly.

He struggled to reconcile the evidence. The thugs had threatened Naomi, demanding their product. She could've used the drugs as payment for the hits on Peter and Henry. But why hide them? If she wasn't using the fentanyl as currency to pay off the men, was she dealing? Like his ex-fiancée, street distribution was the goal. Unless…she was muling it for someone else? He needed to get to the bottom of the mess, but it was a big detour from the RMK. "Let's finish this discussion at the PD. You'll have to come with me."

"What about my van?"

"Douglas County PD will impound it at their lot."

"Great." Naomi groaned. "How am I supposed to work, then?"

She either had a complete disconnect from what he'd just

found, or she was in denial. He was about to arrest her, and she was worried about how she'd fulfill her commitments? Bennett stared at her, gathering his thoughts. She was probably due any day now, but she hadn't slowed down, based on her fourteen-hour, seven-days-a-week tours. Normally, Bennett would've viewed her tenacity as a strong work ethic.

But Naomi wasn't a sweet first-time mother-to-be.

She was a cold-blooded killer.

"Detective Ford, I realize you have no reason to believe me, but I promise you that the drugs aren't mine. I didn't even know they were in there." Naomi maintained her stunned response. "What is it? Cocaine?"

He exhaled an incredulous breath and assumed the cop pose—standing tall, feet shoulder width apart, arms crossed over his chest. "Don't insult my intelligence and yours by playing games with me. You're fully aware a crystal of fentanyl the size of a grain of salt is lethal!"

Naomi gasped, clamping a hand over her mouth. "How did it get under my tour bus? Am I in danger? Is your dog at risk from sniffing it?"

She seemed genuinely concerned. Would a heartless drug dealer be able to fake that?

"No, it's packaged well. Right?"

"I've got no idea."

"We won't take any chances." He moved to his vehicle and withdrew an evidence bag from the toolbox and placed the drugs inside. Bennett secured the evidence in the safe, removed his gloves and returned to where Naomi sat on the crate, holding her head in her hands.

"Naomi, this is your last chance to tell me the truth about it all."

"I can't."

Bennett had assumed she was a serial killer, not a drug dealer. Once more, he berated himself for almost falling for the lies of a beautiful woman. Were the drugs Naomi's actual source of income? Under-the-table dealings that made it appear she was broke on paper? Disdain flowed through him. The familiar situation reminding him of his drug-dealing ex-fiancée, Delaney. "We'll have to finish this discussion at the PD." He reached out a hand, helping her to stand.

Her solemn expression combined with her slumped shoulders, and the exhaustion apparent on her attractive face tugged at a hidden part of Bennett's heart. A stray lock of her thick chestnut brown hair escaped her braid, and she tucked it behind her ear. She paused, placing a hand on the small of her back, clearly worn out. A twinge of sympathy threatened to expose Bennett, and he grunted, actively shoving it away. Sympathy was a weakness in his character that had cost him dearly with Delaney. He'd never go down that road again.

Not now.

Not ever.

Naomi Carr-Cavanaugh was a drug-dealing murderer.

Still, Bennett wondered if the guilt of her crimes weighed on her shoulders. Maybe she wasn't a complete psychopath. Regret for her actions might give her life in prison instead of the alternative. For the sake of her unborn baby, Bennett hoped that was true.

She gasped, gripping her belly. "This can't be happening."

Was she faking labor? Fat chance he'd buy that ruse. "Naomi, I need to read you your rights. You're being arrested for possession of a deadly, controlled substance."

"No. Wait." Her head snapped up, and her skin blanched. "It's not mine."

"Naomi Carr-Cavanaugh, you have the right to remain silent."

She gasped again, crying out in pain. Her knees buckled, and she plunged, digging her nails into his forearm. Her eyes pleaded with him. "Please take me." She heaved. "To the hospital." Another gasp. "I think I'm in labor."

THREE

Naomi inspected the IV line that drooped from her arm. She watched the monitor, relishing the rhythmic beeps and lines reflecting her baby's fetal heart rate. Grateful for the private room, she closed her eyes and prayed for help from the mess that had become her life.

Two raps on the slightly open door preceded Bennett's entrance, ending her prayer time.

"Hey, how're you doing?"

If she wasn't mistaken, he almost appeared uncertain as he entered. Under any other circumstances, that might be touching. Except tonight, she was a suspect, and he was a cop.

"Better." She sat up and Detective Ford hurried to her side, helping to adjust the pillows behind her head. "The contractions are still strong. The doctor said I'm not effaced and only a centimeter dilated."

"It's been a long time since I did obstetric training. Dilate, I remember…" The confused expression on the handsome detective's face implied he needed clarification.

"I have a long way to go before delivery."

He blew out a long breath and pulled a chair closer to her. "Oh."

"They said they'd like to keep me for a while just to make sure. Oh." She gripped the handrails and breathed through the contraction.

He looked a bit overwhelmed and slightly helpless as she practiced her Lamaze breathing technique.

When it finally passed, she exhaled. "Whew!"

He lifted a plastic cup of water, handing it to her. "Has this happened before?"

"Contractions?"

He nodded.

"Nope, this was my first time. Of course, I'm also new to this pregnancy thing, so every event sort of happens unexpectedly." She took a sip, considering the personal feel of their conversation. If only she could forget she was a suspect. Facing him, she addressed why he sat beside her. "You have no reason to believe me, and I have no way to prove my innocence. I've never used—" she glanced past him to make sure the door was closed and whispered "—drugs."

He looked over his shoulder. "Why are you whispering?"

Her cheeks warmed. "It's embarrassing to have this discussion."

The corner of his lips tilted upward. Did she amuse him?

"Anyway, nor do I associate with anyone who uses them." She sniffed. "Who am I kidding? I don't associate with anyone outside of my tour customers, period."

"No friends?"

"Acquaintances, but nothing beyond that. After Ted's death, I buried myself in my job. I have bigger fish to fry, as they say." She rubbed her belly for emphasis. "This little man is my biggest and most important priority. I'd never endanger or risk losing him. Especially not for something like that."

"I don't say this lightly. I want to believe you, but your word isn't enough."

Naomi glanced past the detective, refusing to let her emotions take hold of her again.

"You're in possession of illegal narcotics. I cannot ignore that." He leaned back in the chair. "It's against protocol."

Naomi opened her mouth to protest, then closed it. "I understand." Wasn't the saying possession was nine-tenths of the law?

He tilted his head.

"Why are you looking at me that way?"

"Rarely do people surprise me, Naomi." He met her gaze, and for the first time, she noticed the light brown color of his eyes. "I expected a knock-down-drag-out fight with you."

"Sorry." She lifted her hands in mock surrender. "I'm too tired. The hits just keep on coming, and I'm running out of energy to battle the world, Detective Ford."

"At this point, let's shift to a first-name basis," he said. "Please call me Bennett."

"Bennett." She tried the name, concluding it fit him well. "Is that protocol?" she quipped.

"No, definitely not. Having my suspect go into labor while I'm trying to arrest her is new for me."

She offered him a slight grin. "Where is Spike?"

"They wouldn't let him in with me, so one of the hospital security guards was kind enough to take him until we're released."

"Oh, that was nice. But you don't have to stay here."

He guffawed. "Um, yes, I do. We have unfinished business."

"Right." She slid further down in the bed, warring with the urge to pull the blankets over her head and hide from her waking nightmare.

"I also called the Douglas County Sheriff's Department and requested they pick up your van. It'll be in their impound lot."

"Great." She rolled her eyes. "One more thing to pay for and deal with."

"Since we're killing time—" Bennett lifted one foot, resting it on his knee in a figure-four position "—let's discuss you and Peter."

"I was shocked and brokenhearted to learn of his...death." Naomi fidgeted with the blanket. "Sad too that we didn't talk more. He came to see me when I first moved here."

"Is he the reason you relocated to Denver?"

"No, this was my husband Ted's hometown." Naomi glanced at the baby monitor again. "When he brought me here to research ideas for our tour business, I fell in love with Colorado."

"I get that. I've seen beautiful places, but I was glad to be back on my home turf for this case." Bennett took another cup, pouring water from the plastic pitcher. "Kind of makes me protective of it."

Naomi nodded, unsure what he meant by the comment.

"You returned to Peter's ranch to reminisce about him?" Something in his question told Naomi he was fishing for more.

When she'd apparently taken too long to respond, he said, "I have assumptions, but I'd prefer your side of the story." His posture softened. "Naomi, I explained I'm with the MCK9 task force. We're searching for the Rocky Mountain Killer. The person responsible for the deaths of Seth Jenkins, Brad Kingsley, Aaron Anderson, Peter Windham and Henry Mulder."

"I still can't believe a serial killer murdered my former classmates."

"I'm sure you understand there are several common factors linking the cases. You were recent graduates of Elk Valley High School involved in the Young Ranchers Club, and you all attended the semiformal ten years ago."

"We weren't the only people fitting that criterion."

"Except you're the one cohesive portion."

"What?" Naomi's head whipped upward. "Why? I knew all the victims—past and present. That's no secret to anyone."

"Hey, I get why someone would think those young men had it coming to them. What they did to you at the dance was incomprehensible. I can't even imagine the pain they caused you. The humiliation." Something in his eyes conveyed honesty in the statement.

"What they did was horrible and mean, but to retaliate by killing the people who bullied them?"

"Happens more than you'd believe."

"That was ages ago. I don't cling to the past."

"But they define us." Bennett leaned forward, elbows on his knees. "Experiences good and bad change us. Mine did."

What did that mean? "Experiences don't define our identity. They help us grow and learn. If we're willing. Are you a man of faith, Bennett?"

He hesitated. Was he reluctant to answer her or not willing to share anything about himself? Finally, he said, "Yes. But my faith has changed over the years, too."

"As it should. I believe God uses everything—good, bad, and indifferent—to mold our character. I trust Him to redeem even the bad stuff. I can't spend valuable time and effort nursing grudges and holding on to past anger."

"I suppose that's true. Except five of the individuals who were connected to the prank are dead. That goes beyond coincidence."

Unable to rebut that, she remained silent.

"How did you find out about Peter and Henry's murders?"

"I don't live in a cave," she said, tilting her head. "News travels fast with the internet, and my brother, Evan, still lives and owns a business in Elk Valley. He told me." She swallowed hard. "I was sad to hear about Henry. Nobody deserves to die the way they did. But Peter's demise hurt me the most. He was always kind to me."

"He wasn't on the night of the prank. A friend would've warned or protected."

Naomi looked down. "He didn't participate in the prank."

"That's a compassionate attitude."

"Peter and his friends went everywhere together. Acted like they're invincible, and all had reputations for dating multiple girls. Have you considered the possibility that they played pranks on other students, too?" Naomi's question seemed to hit home.

"It's possible," Bennett replied.

"Be assured, I've had more than enough excitement and difficulty over the past year that I don't need to invite trouble."

"Are you speaking of your husband's death?"

Naomi hesitated, momentarily taken aback by his obvious research into her life. "Yes. Losing Ted—" her voice cracked, but she quickly recovered "—and trying to keep up with the bills and our tour company while growing another human being is a lot."

He nodded. "Financial pressure is a reason for many crimes."

"I'm surviving."

"Here's my take on what happened. Those young men had to pay for what they did to you. The first three murders happened on Valentine's Day a year ago. You sent them the message, asking to meet at the barn, then took them out one by one."

"I did not!" Naomi bolted upright in the bed. "I don't own a gun. Check my alibi! I wasn't anywhere near the barn the night of Seth's, Brad's and Aaron's deaths."

"Hmm." He appeared nonplussed. Was he listening?

"Evan will vouch for me. I was home on Valentine's Day. He was there comforting me while I bawled my eyes out. I felt stupid for falling for the prank. I had a huge crush on Trevor Gage, and I was giddy when he asked me out. I'd watched all the teen romance movies and naively assumed the dance would be the beginning of something wonderful between us. Evan stayed with me until he left to pick up his girlfriend, Paulina."

"Paulina Potter?" Bennett clarified.

"Yes, and they went on their big night out."

"That leaves a gap where you could've committed the murders."

Naomi fisted her hands. "I worked the late shift at the hospice in Elk Valley."

He withdrew a notepad from his shirt pocket. "What time was that?"

"Nine p.m. to two a.m. I was in a building full of nurses and patients that night. Check the records."

"That's helpful. Thank you."

His willingness to consider her alibi prompted Naomi to continue. "I was in ninety-nine-year-old Annie Perkin's room from eleven p.m. to one fifteen a.m." Naomi hadn't reminisced about Annie in ages. "Such a sweet lady." The details returned, motivating her to speak faster. "Her nurse came in at midnight to check her vitals. Annie pleaded for me to stay with her. She was dying and didn't want to be alone."

"What was her nurse's name?" Bennett's pen hovered over his notepad.

Naomi traversed her recollections. "Yvette Jacobsen. Annie had dozed off and Yvette stayed with me for a while. We talked about her son and his recent move to San Diego for college. Feel free to call her, too."

"Okay. We'll dig into that."

"See, that clears me and proves I didn't kill anyone."

"Well, it's an alibi for the first three murders, but not for those of Henry Mulder and Peter Windham." He tapped his pen against the notebook paper.

Several seconds ticked by before Naomi gaped at him. "Wait. Are you still implying that I killed Peter and Henry?" She gestured at her belly. "In my current condition? You must be kidding. Look at me!" She swept her arms wide. "I'm nine months pregnant. I'm a human duck waddling around. How would I murder two grown men?"

Bennett's tone remained calm. "You had cause, arguably justifiable cause for revenge, and realistically, physical strength isn't required to fire a gun."

"Again, I don't own a gun, nor do I know how to use one." She fought to maintain a controlled persona. She'd not give the detective the satisfaction of seeing her fall apart at his questioning.

Bennett exhaled.

Naomi's heart thudded against her chest in frustration, and

another contraction hit. She repeated the breathing exercises until it passed.

"I'm not here to upset you, Naomi. But without facts, like the alibi at the hospice, I have nowhere to look." He leaned forward again.

"Detective, I assume you've followed me for a while. Otherwise, I'm not sure how you found me at Peter's."

He held his place, one hand on the bed. "Yes."

"Then you're aware I work from sunrise to sunset. Once I finish my tours, I'm exhausted and every part of my body hurts. Hauling and growing another human requires substantial effort." Naomi wrapped her hands over her belly.

"I can't argue those facts."

"Not that I'd expect you to understand. I don't have the time, energy or inclination to hunt down people from my past." Naomi sat up. "Check my tour bus records. I use a computer application." She spelled the name of the program, providing the login and password for him.

Bennett wrote the details in his notebook.

"You'll see I've had a full schedule for months. I don't get time off, and even if I did, I can't afford to take it." She sucked in a breath and paused.

He met her gaze, concern etching his forehead.

"My husband cleaned out my bank accounts, and I have yet to find the money. I must work for a living, which impedes on my opportunities to commit murder. Therefore, I am not the serial killer you're seeking."

"I appreciate your candidness." Bennett pocketed the notepad and sat back. Was he finished interrogating her? "Should I call someone to let them know you're here?"

"You mean as in my one phone call when you book me?" She'd meant the statement sarcastically, but it fell flat.

If she hadn't imagined it, he almost seemed to cringe.

"I'll save it for calling my brother if and or when that becomes necessary."

He nodded. "Tell me about your brother, Evan? Does he visit often?"

Apparently not. "He comes to visit me twice a year." Naomi shrugged. "Evan's the best. Every little sister probably says that. We've never been especially close. Since the death of our folks, even seeing him is hard on me. Without those connections to my past, I can forget parts of the pain and loss. But each of those reminders makes it all fresh."

"Did you receive the invitation to the Elk Valley High reunion?"

"Yes. Why?"

"I imagine receiving that brought back those old memories. Created the catalyst for finishing off the men who hurt you. You were all graduates of Elk Valley High."

Naomi's patience waned. "As I explained, Detective, I have bigger things on my mind than taking revenge for a stupid prank at a dance." She turned away. "It's been a long day and I'm exhausted. I'd like to rest."

"Sure." He stood. "I'll play it straight with you, Mrs. Carr-Cavanaugh. You had motive, opportunity and means. The MOM method, as we'd say."

The acronym seemed especially cruel now. "Detective, that's true of a lot of people. If you had evidence, you wouldn't waste time following me. Now, with all due respect, sir, either arrest me or let me sleep." She didn't wait for him to respond. She rolled over, facing the baby monitor machine, and closed her eyes.

Bennett shut Naomi's door softly behind him and walked toward the waiting room at the far end of the hall. Relieved to enter the empty space, he sat positioned with a good visual of Naomi's door.

"Might as well make some more calls," he mumbled, glancing down, half expecting to see Spike. Talking to himself appeared less strange when his K-9 partner accompanied him.

Bennett chuckled, withdrew his phone and dialed the MCK9 teammate tech specialist, Isla Jimenez.

She answered on the second ring. "Hey, Bennett."

"How's it going?"

"Depends on what we're discussing."

Bennett assumed Isla referenced the foster parent approval process she was enduring. At their last discussion, she'd told him there was an infant they were placing with her. "Any word on when you'll get the baby?"

"Not yet. I'm grateful for the busyness of this case to keep me occupied. Otherwise, I'd spend every waking moment biting my nails and walking on pins and super-excited-can't-wait-for-the-phone-to-ring needles."

"I'm sure it'll happen soon." Bennett grinned at the enthusiasm in her voice. "You must be their poster child candidate for what a great foster parent should be."

"I pray you're right." Isla laughed. "What's up?"

"So much I'm not sure where to start. I have interesting information to share about Naomi Carr-Cavanaugh." He paused, considering how differently her name sounded on his lips than it had in the beginning. The one-dimensional cardboard Naomi had become three dimensional. When had that happened?

Knock it off, Ford. He shook off the thoughts. No. She remained a suspect until they confirmed or destroyed her alibis for the murders. Thus, the need to involve Isla.

"Ready when you are." Her voice prompted him, reminding Bennett he'd stalled too long.

"Here's the rundown." He withdrew the notebook where he'd written the details Naomi provided.

"Bring it on."

Bennett conveyed Naomi's story about sitting with the hospice patient on the night of the first murders. "I could be wrong, but it seems plausible. She was confident Yvette Jacobsen would corroborate her alibi."

"Should be easy to verify that information," she replied, and tapping filled the line. "I'll check the hospice facility records and get back to you."

"There's more," Bennett replied. "She claimed to run a full tour bus schedule since before Ted's death. If that's true, she also has an alibi for the last two homicides."

"Hmm, any chance she told you which online scheduling program she uses?"

"Yes." Bennett read off the details.

"That's an older app. Stand by." More tapping. "I'll dig into the calendar and contact her customers to verify they were on her tours at the times of the homicides," Isla confirmed. "I'll be in touch."

After they'd disconnected, Bennett called FBI Wyoming Bureau supervisory special agent Chase Rawlston, the appointed leader to the task force. "Hey, Bennett."

"It's been an adventurous night." Bennett launched into a detailed but concise synopsis of the evening, including the shooting, Spike's drug find and the events leading up to the hospital visit.

"You went from zero to sixty in a single night," Chase replied. "How is Naomi doing?"

"They have her in a private room, monitoring the contractions. Apparently, she's not effaced or dilated, which means she won't deliver soon. The doctor wants to keep her for a while to make sure."

Chase chuckled. "You're getting an education in obstetrics."

"Affirmative." Bennett dropped into a chair. "I planned to cite and arrest her for possession, but then she started having contractions, and now we're at the hospital."

"Understandable," Chase said.

"There's more. She has reasonable alibis for all the murders. Isla's checking out the details, but I've got doubts about her involvement as the RMK."

"Put a pin in that until Isla contacts you," Chase replied. "Regardless, her alibis don't explain the drugs."

"Agreed, and I'm not inclined to just let that go, but I'm struggling to reconcile the chain of events."

"You're doubtful the drugs belong to Naomi?" Chase asked.

"I don't know." Bennett leaned back in the seat and ran a hand over his hair. Chase knew his history with Delaney, so he was grateful he didn't need to explain that or his hesitancy to trust his instincts. "I can't tell you how many times someone's claimed they're holding drugs for a friend or relative. Or they plead ignorance. Something is different about her."

"Talk it out with me."

"If she's the RMK, why drive to the crime scene with narcotics? That's a risky move all by itself."

"Or Naomi drove there to heighten the thrill of getting away with murder. She celebrated by meeting her accomplices to deliver the fentanyl."

"True." Bennett paused. "Why not meet them in a clandestine place? For the record, I'm not convinced those men were working for or with her. They both wore ski masks. Why hide their identities?"

"Yeah," Chase grunted. "That's strange."

"Exactly. And get this, she blushed and whispered the word *drug* as though she was worried someone might overhear her."

"That's easily explained. She is in the hospital, pregnant and close to delivery," Chase responded. "She's right to worry a nurse would eavesdrop on the conversation, putting her in danger of losing custody of her baby."

"I hate when you're logical," Bennett said. Once more, he'd lost focus. Another perfect example of why he needed his team to keep him unbiased.

"Nah, you're in the thick of the investigation. Helps to talk it out and gain some perspective," Chase replied. "Sometimes the logic is right in front of us. Other times, it's masked by circumstances."

Or Bennett's inability to read through the lies spoken by a

beautiful woman. "I'd feel better if more of the details added up, especially regarding the drugs."

"Unless the shooters trailed you trailing Naomi. Doubtful since they didn't try to take you out before attacking her. How'd they know she'd be there?"

"Can't argue that." Even though he wanted to. "There's something more going on here. If she is the RMK, the drugs are important but not the goal." Bennett ran a hand over his head. "Would you allow me to release her for medical reasons with the citation for possession while we run the bags for DNA and fingerprints?"

"Approved. I don't see Naomi as a flight risk."

Bennett exhaled relief, though he wasn't sure why. Didn't he want to arrest Naomi? No, he wanted to take down the RMK. Stopping any distribution of fentanyl was important, but not the goal. Either way, he wouldn't fall for another innocent woman act. She remained a suspect he was keeping a close eye on. That was all. "Thanks."

"Get the evidence transferred to Isla ASAP, and we'll find out what's going on," Chase said.

"With your permission, to expedite results, I respectfully request utilizing local resources to process the evidence. I've got a great contact at a Colorado lab here that the Denver PD uses."

"As long as your highest priority is maintaining a tight chain of custody," Chase replied. "And include Isla in all communication."

"Roger that. Douglas County is the responding agency for the Windham Ranch incident. I'll follow up with them as soon as we disconnect. I want Spike to go through Naomi's vehicle again to confirm we didn't miss anything the first time." Bennett couldn't shake his skepticism that Naomi faked the contractions to prevent him from finding more drugs.

"Good plan. Keep me updated."

Talking with Chase triggered something in the back of his mind about Naomi's involvement. Once Denver PD tested the bags for DNA or fingerprints, he'd feel better. If she'd hidden the fentanyl, he doubted she'd bothered to do so wearing gloves. Additionally, if they found her fingerprints on the bags, he'd have more evidence to prove she was dealing drugs.

"Is that everything you needed to tell me?"

"I think so," Bennett replied.

"My turn," Chase said. "Should've looped you in sooner, but things are hectic on this end, too."

Bennett's full attention shifted to his boss.

"Cowgirl is missing."

"Say again?" Bennett gaped at the phone, unsure he'd understood Chase. The cute Labradoodle had been gifted to the task force to train as an emotional support dog for their investigation.

"Liana was outside with Cowgirl in the training center. She thought she heard gunfire and turned to look for a shooter. Liana called for backup, and when she finished talking to the dispatcher, Cowgirl was gone. She saw a man in black running away, but he vanished into the woods."

"Unbelievable. Why take her?" Bennett muttered. "Didn't Liana hear her barking?"

"We're not sure exactly what happened. Liana's taking full responsibility. There's no way she could've predicted this would happen. Cowgirl never barked, at least not to Liana's recollection. But that's not a surprise. She loves everyone."

"Oh, wow." Bennett thought about his teammate, Ashley Hanson, a cop in Elk Valley and the youngest member of the MCK9 task force. An emotional support dog had been Ashley's great idea, and her dad, an FBI bigwig in DC, had gifted her to the team. "How's Ashley holding up?"

"She's determined to find Cowgirl, like the rest of us."

"Is there anything I can do?" Why hadn't they told him sooner? Team communication was essential.

"We've searched the area and have feelers out for any sightings to be reported straight to the MCK9 task force. It's a local job, and that's part of the reason I didn't race to tell you." Chase's comment answered Bennett's unspoken question. "I need your undivided attention focused on Naomi and the investigation there. Selena and Kyle are returning to Colorado to assist in the investigation. They'll be in touch soon. Between all of you, I'm hoping we'll find what we need to stop the RMK from taking any more lives."

"Affirmative."

Once they'd disconnected, Bennett glanced down at his phone and sent a silent prayer for Cowgirl's quick and safe return. He called the Douglas County Sheriff's Department. The dispatcher provided him a case number and connected him directly to the deputy assigned to Naomi's van.

"Deputy McClintock," she answered on the second ring.

"This is Detective Bennett Ford with the Mountain Country K-9 Task Force. I was advised you're handling the processing of evidence from the Windham shooting incident."

"Yes, sir. Sorry for the delay in getting out there. It's been a busy day."

"Understandable. I'm at the hospital with the owner of the van," he said. "Would it be possible to get an update?"

"Not much to share. I handled the transportation and impounding of Mrs. Carr-Cavanaugh's vehicle. The shooter did quite a number on it. Other than severe cosmetic damage, strangely, it's still running. We've also collected casings."

"I appreciate that." The deputy's response sounded a little dramatic compared to what he'd seen, but then maybe she'd not had as much experience with shootings as he had over the years. "Would you please transfer the evidence to my contact at Denver PD? He'll handle the processing for our team."

"Absolutely."

Bennett provided Deputy McClintock DPD's crime lab technician Eduardo Gomez's information. "I'd also like to have my K-9 go through the van again once the doctor releases Mrs. Carr-Cavanaugh."

"Not a problem. Just advise the case number and show your credentials to the guard at the entrance if I'm not here."

"Thank you."

Bennett disconnected and got to his feet. He strolled through the hallway, where cheerful baby decorations filled the space. When he reached Naomi's door, he rapped softly. He got no response and gently pushed open the door.

Naomi lay on her side, eyes closed, breathing evenly.

He retreated and walked back to the empty waiting room. His cell phone vibrated as he sat down.

Isla's contact information popped up on his screen.

The moment of truth.

Bennett swiped to answer. "What do you have for me?"

FOUR

Naomi glanced around the hospital room, relieved she was alone, then checked her cell phone on the bed table. She'd napped for more than an hour. No sign of the detective. Good. Maybe Bennett Ford had gone home and given her a reprieve from his incessant interrogation.

Ted's appreciation for nonstop crime shows made her wary of the detective's antics. He'd been tough with her, then befriended her, intending to bait Naomi into confessing she'd killed Peter and the others. She'd recognized his unrelenting determination, etched like the rigid lines in his expression. He believed Naomi was a murderer. After the fact, the urge to remain silent and contact a lawyer had occurred to her. She'd probably talked too much in her resolve to set the record straight.

How did I get into this mess, Lord?

Tears threatened. She'd faked sleep in a cowardly effort not to face her accuser when the detective had returned to her room. After all she'd endured in the past six months, this was one more thing to deal with, and she didn't have the energy.

The fetal heart rate monitor chimed softly, filling Naomi with worry. If Ford arrested her, what would happen to her son?

As soon as the detective mentioned the Elk Valley High School reunion, Naomi discerned what had drawn her to Peter's ranch. Zoe Jenkins's invitation. A part of Naomi wanted to attend, but only as an observer. The greater temptation was to light the invitation on fire and pretend she'd never received it.

Without her consent, Naomi's thoughts traveled to the night of the dance and the incident Detective Bennett claimed gave her the motive to kill. She'd fallen prey to Trevor Gage by her own childish, impossible crush. How ridiculous to believe the town's golden boy would want anything to do with someone like her. But when Trevor asked her to the dance, she'd practically jumped out of her skin with delight. She'd spent all day getting ready and arrived with stars in her eyes. Until Trevor's pack humiliated her and she'd run home crying. Her only happy memory of that night was Evan's attempts to console her.

She thought about the note the killer had left stabbed in their chests. Didn't it say something about how they deserved it? Trevor's despicable friends had triggered someone's murderous hatred. Except sweet, thoughtful Peter wasn't like them. Whether he'd participated in the prank to any degree, and she doubted he had, he was her friend. She'd preferred his company over the snobby girls who befriended her, only to reject her on a dime.

Naomi caught her reflection in the fetal monitor, revealing the rat's nest her hair had become. She pushed herself upright in the bed, tugged off her hair tie and then finger-combed the strands. Another unwelcome memory returned, reminding Naomi of an incident in the school bathroom. She normally avoided going in when the cheerleaders were there, but they'd come in after her, and she was cornered. One of them, whose name escaped Naomi's mind, had rudely suggested Naomi color her hair to get rid of the "mousy bland brown" to blond or red. Until that moment, Naomi had liked her hair. When she told her mother about the comment, she'd brushed her long locks, cooing about the color, soft and tawny, like a fawn. Sorrow constricted Naomi's heart.

She gasped at little man's impatient kick to the ribs. "You're right. That was a long time ago." Her hand gently stroked the place where her infant's foot pressed against her skin. "Thank you for the reminder, Lord," she prayed aloud.

Talking with the detective reactivated too many buried memories that refused to be ignored. She'd never regretted moving away from Wyoming and starting a life in Colorado with Ted. Even with the assortment of abundant troubles toward the end of their marriage, she was grateful for the pleasant years they'd had before things spiraled downhill. She'd cling to those and not the sad parts. As Daddy would've said, *Too much hindsight masks the future in could've-beens.*

Her thoughts shifted to the last couple from her evening tour. They were kind, as Naomi imagined her parents would've been, had the car accident not cut their lives short. They'd regaled her with tales of their eight children and fifteen grandchildren. The woman had shared excruciating details of delivering each of her babies. Naomi grinned. She could have done without that.

It happened more often than not. Strangers found it necessary to share their gruesome birthing experiences and attempted to rub her belly while she was standing in line at the store. As though she wore a giant sign with Pet Me on it.

Naomi chuckled softly. She loved talking with her customers. Since Ted's absences were masked as busyness at first, then marital separation and subsequent death, the silence in her home was deafening. "You'll fix that, though. Won't you, sweetie?" She cooed, rubbing her taut belly.

Her son wriggled in agreement with two quick kicks. "Come on, little man, I know you're squished in there but that's not fun for mommy."

Soon, the months of loneliness would end, and she'd hold her precious gift from God. Tears stung her eyes. Unless Detective Ford arrested her for murder and charged her with possessing illegal narcotics.

Why would someone hide drugs in her van? If she couldn't get the detective to listen to her and search for the truth, how would she convince him of her innocence? Would the charges alone cost Naomi her baby? The tour bus company? Would she lose her license?

Naomi's pulse increased, and the fetal monitor beeped, reminding her of the urgency.

Her life had spun out of control.

The door opened, jolting her to the moment. An unfamiliar man entered, then pushed the door closed. He was tall, and the white doctor's jacket he wore over blue scrubs seemed too tight against his husky stature. He wore bulky, dark-rimmed glasses. A surgical mask covered the lower half of his face, but the menacing look in his dark eyes bore through Naomi. A small scar trailed over his left eyebrow, deep and thick.

Her instincts blared. This was no doctor.

Naomi gasped, leaning hard against the pillow. Her hand slapped at the bed coverings, seeking the call button remote.

At last, her fingers grazed the thick cord.

The device hung on the side of her bed.

Out of reach.

Naomi maintained eye contact with the intruder while inching the remote closer. It thwacked the bed rails, demanding his attention.

"I wouldn't do that if I were you." He closed the distance between them in two long strides.

"What…what…do you want?" Naomi's stammered question exposed her fear.

"Only what belongs to me." The man's voice was a deep growl, vicious and terrifying. He stepped closer, blocking her escape, and lifted his hand. The light bounced off the large blade he produced from his doctor's jacket. "Scream, and it'll be the last sound you ever make."

Naomi swallowed hard, instinctively moving her hands to cover her belly.

A rapping on the door caught their attention. The man spun as though unsure what to do. He backed up, placed a finger against his lips and ducked into the bathroom, hidden from sight.

Naomi was certain he was watching.

Another rap on the door.

"Come in," she squeaked.

The kind nurse who had spent most of the visit attending to Naomi entered, leaving the door ajar. "Time for another check. If you haven't made any progress, the doctor will release you. Then you can chalk this adventure up to Braxton-Hicks contractions."

Naomi's throat went dry. How could she warn the nurse without endangering them both?

In response to her unspoken question, she spotted the man surreptitiously slipping out of the room, undetected.

Bennett exited the restroom and dodged to the right to avoid colliding with a young man sprinting around the corner. "Whoa," Bennett said.

"Sorry. I'm looking for room 242. They admitted my wife already and it's our first baby and I'm all turned around." The man's rapid-fire speech paused for a second.

"It's behind you. The numbers go up from here. You want the other hallway." Bennett gestured to the closed double doors separating the hospital's new wing.

"Great. Thanks." The man spun on his heel and hurried past Bennett.

After making a ridiculous number of laps around the waiting area to force himself to stay awake, Bennett had the hospital layout memorized.

He walked toward Naomi's room. He'd done his best to give her the rest she'd needed. The last thing he wanted was to be the reason she went into early labor. He reached Naomi's door, nearly colliding with the on-call female doctor approaching from the hallway to his left. "Hi there. I'm headed in to examine Mrs. Carr-Cavanaugh."

Bennett wasn't sure what that entailed, but he felt confident Naomi wouldn't appreciate him intruding in on that moment. "Oh, I uh…" Words failed him.

"You can come in with me or wait until she's finished, whichever you're more comfortable with," the doctor said.

Grateful for the excuse, he replied, "I'll wait out here."

"No problem. I'll wave you in when I'm done."

Bennett took the opportunity to call Isla while observing Naomi's door. Not that he'd expected the shooters to follow them to the hospital, but instincts said to remain vigilant.

He dialed Isla's number. "What's up, Bennett?"

"I'm killing time and thought I'd check in. Any progress on confirming the alibis?"

"I'm close. So far, she checks out, but I should have it completed by this evening," Isla replied. "Just waiting for the hospice records to come through. Talk soon."

The line disconnected before Bennett responded. He glanced at the phone. That wasn't like Isla, but he'd swamped her with information. Add that to the RMK investigation and Cowgirl's missing status, and Isla's shortness was explainable.

From the end of the hall, Bennett spotted the doctor waving him over. "All finished."

He rose and went to Naomi's room, rapping on the door.

"Come in," Naomi called.

He entered to find her fully dressed except for her shoes. "They're springing you, huh?" As soon as the words escaped his lips, he longed to erase them.

Naomi's eyes widened, and she swallowed hard. She looked as though she wanted to respond, but the nurse returned with discharge orders in her hand. "You're a free woman."

Ugh. They'd both chosen the wrong words.

Naomi averted her gaze. "I'm embarrassed."

"Don't be, honey. I had awful Braxton-Hicks contractions with my first. They'll tell you they're just uncomfortable." The nurse grunted good-naturedly. "Not hardly. Enough to bring me to my knees." She winked at Naomi, then addressed Bennett. "Make sure she drinks lots of water and gets plenty of rest."

She patted him on the shoulder. "I'm sure you'll be wonderful parents." She exited the room.

Bennett's face warmed.

"Sorry," Naomi whispered. "I didn't know what to say when they assumed you were my husband."

Husband. It had been a long time since he'd even entertained the thought of sharing his life with someone. He studied Naomi, and though he had reason to be irritated, he wasn't. What was wrong with him? "It's fine. Easier than saying I'm your arresting officer."

"Right."

He helped her with her shoes. "I have good news and bad news."

Fear complicated her inquisitive expression. "Okay."

"Good news first, my commander has authorized me to cite you for possession with a medical release."

"Guess that's better than going to jail."

"I'll give you a ride home." He wasn't taking any chances she'd try to get into her van.

"What about my van?" she asked as though reading this mind.

"That's the bad news. Douglas County Sheriff's Department impounded it, and it's too late to get in there tonight."

"I'll cancel my tours for tomorrow." Naomi hung her head. "I'll have to refund everyone's money unless I can get Addy to cover for me."

"Who is that?"

"Adeline Everett owns Mile High Town Tours." Naomi exhaled. "My competitor."

Bennett wrote the name on his notepad, intending to ask Isla to follow up on it later. "Are you friends?"

"Sort of," Naomi replied. "More like frenemies. It's a complicated relationship."

"How so?"

"We offer the same services and comparable prices, which

puts us on opposite ends of the competitive spectrum." She tilted her head. "At the same time, she's the perfect one to help in situations like this. And we've worked out an agreement for when the baby comes."

Bennett considered the information. Would Addy have reason to eliminate Naomi's business? "Does she get all the profit? She'll be doing the work, but she's also getting your customers."

"Most of the profit. We agreed on an eighty-twenty split." Naomi shrugged. "It's better than nothing when I'm unable to work."

The agreement didn't seem fair to Bennett. Addy was taking advantage of Naomi's vulnerability, especially if she'd booked the tours prior. But what did he know about the tour business? He quirked a brow and tucked the notepad into his pocket.

Bennett might sympathize with Naomi, except he wasn't the one who'd hidden illegal drugs. "I need to pick up Spike," he said, diverting the conversation before he offered to comfort a possible criminal. He held open the door, allowing her to exit first.

Then he led her down the hallway to the elevators.

"Can I go with you?" Naomi's demeanor had changed. She seemed skittish, hugging her purse close to her body.

"Of course. Is something wrong?"

"What? Why?" She spun to look behind her.

"Because you're a little jumpy."

What had happened in the time she'd spent in her room? Had she had nightmares? Did the person she was holding the drugs for contact her? Irritation wove through him. He'd considered the possibility of her innocence in this mess. Once more, he was wrong.

They wordlessly walked to the security office on the main level. A large sign posted on the closed door instructed them to push the buzzer for assistance. Bennett depressed the button, which emitted a horrendous buzz that must've startled

Naomi, because she jerked and bumped into him with an apologetic grimace.

A speaker beside the door crackled to life. "Security."

"Detective Bennett Ford."

A click announced the lock had released. Bennett turned the knob and pushed the heavy door open. Naomi shifted close behind him. Spike lounged on the loveseat at the far side of the office. At Bennett's entrance, the beagle jumped up on all fours, wagging his whole body.

Bennett couldn't contain his smile. "Hey, buddy."

"Detective," the security officer greeted from his seat in front of a series of computer monitors.

Bennett struggled to remember the guy's name. Ben? Bert? He shifted to the side, glimpsing the badge. Bill Nolice. "Thanks again."

"It was a joy." Nolice smiled broadly.

Spike rushed and jumped into Bennett's outstretched arms. Nolice chuckled. "He's happy to see you."

"The feeling's mutual." Bennett set Spike down and snapped on his leash.

The stout man rose, keeping one hand on the chair. "I enjoyed his company."

"He's great if you don't have drugs on you." Bennett ruffled the dog's fur, catching Naomi's wince in his peripheral vision. Stuck between feeling like a heel and the satisfaction of reestablishing their roles, he averted his eyes. "Let's get going."

"Have a good night." Nolice offered Naomi a nod.

She returned a tired half smile.

They exited the security office and walked silently to where his pickup was parked.

Once they'd driven away from the hospital, Naomi said, "I need to tell you something."

At last, she'd confess. "Okay." Bennett slowed and pulled the truck over to the side of the road.

"No! Keep going!" Naomi twisted around to look behind them. "He might follow us."

"Who?"

"Drive and I'll talk."

Bennett accelerated.

"A man threatened me in my room."

Bennett slammed on the brakes, stretching his right arm to cover Naomi in an involuntary protective maneuver. "What?" He searched the parking lot and road for any approaching vehicles.

"Not here. It was before the doctor released me." Naomi waved her arms. "Go!"

Against his better judgment, Bennett continued driving from the hospital. "You should've told me sooner!"

"Why didn't you stop him from getting into my room?"

Bennett's head snapped back from the verbal slap. "I watched your room the entire time we were there. The only distraction I'd had was almost getting run over by a soon-to-be-dad."

Understanding poured over Naomi's face, illuminated by the truck's interior dashboard lights.

"Please start from the beginning."

"I awoke right before a man entered my room. He wore scrubs and a doctor's coat, and a mask covered his mouth. There was a big thick scar over his left eye. I didn't suspect anything until he got closer. I could feel hate rolling off him in waves." Naomi exhaled. "He held a knife. He warned me not to make a sound and demanded I give him 'what belongs to him.' Then the nurse knocked on the door. He hid in the attached bathroom. I was terrified he'd burst out and stab her!" Naomi's words ended on a quivering note.

Bennett reached a hand to comfort her. She'd put someone else's life ahead of her own?

"I'm sorry." Her voice trembled. "I wasn't sure if he'd stayed at the hospital watching us. I wanted to get out of there alive."

"We'll need to review the hospital security footage." Bennett pulled over and called Isla.

"I don't know if we've ever talked this many times in one day," Isla said, but the teasing words didn't match her sharp tone.

"Hey, is everything okay?"

"No. We'll talk later. What's up?"

Concern for his teammate had Bennett pausing, but he wouldn't press her with Naomi freaking out beside him. "I need to get access to the security footage from the hospital." He relayed the information Naomi had shared, including the description of the intruder. "Also add Adeline Everett to your background search. She's a colleague of Naomi's."

"On it."

"Thanks."

They disconnected, and Bennett shifted into Drive. "I wish you'd told me all of this at the hospital."

"I was scared and seriously considered running away, except you'd have labeled me a fugitive serial killer slash drug dealer." She gave him a weak smile.

"I'm glad you didn't run. And this explains why you were so jumpy."

Naomi didn't cease to surprise him, but anger at his ineptness in missing the intruder's appearance boiled his blood.

Naomi's voice trembled. "He threatened to kill me and demanded his stuff."

Bennett wanted to reprimand her for withholding the information, but her justification made sense. "Wait, what did you say?"

"He said he wanted what belongs to him."

"Do you think he meant the drugs in your van or something else?" An icy shiver trickled down Bennett's back. Had he recovered everything from the van? Or was there something more hidden there? And if so, what?

"That's what I'm assuming."

Bennett checked the dashboard clock. The impound lot was closed. Surely, someone guarded the premises. One look at Naomi, and the exhaustion she wore concerned Bennett. He couldn't drag her out there at this hour, anyway. "Naomi, please use my phone to call Deputy McClintock and put it on speakerphone."

She did as he asked. The deputy answered on the third ring, sounding less than pleased with his late-night interruption. "Deputy McClintock."

"I apologize for calling at this time of night, but there's been a recent development in the case I'm working on. Does the impound lot have twenty-four-hour security?"

"Yes, both a full-time guard and security cameras."

"My K-9 and I will go over the van first thing in the morning."

"I'll notify the guard."

"Thank you," Bennett said.

Naomi took the phone and swiped to hang up. "What're you thinking?"

"I want to find anything left in the van before they do."

FIVE

The ride to Naomi's home was silent for many reasons. None of which helped her current predicament if she bothered striking up a conversation.

"It's the end building." Before Naomi finished speaking the words, Bennett had already headed in the direction where she'd pointed. Of course, he was familiar with the area if he'd followed her. Irritation rose within her at the realization.

He parked in front of her two-story townhome. A bright colorful wreath decorated with plastic Easter eggs hung askew on the front door. As if seeing the decoration for the first time, Naomi realized the holiday had passed two weeks ago. She'd come and gone, scarcely noticing it or the fact that a detective had surveilled her. Her extended work hours had melted into one continuous day, making them indistinguishable from one another.

Bennett shut off the engine and faced her. "I need to leash Spike before we head inside."

Naomi didn't argue. It was pointless to do so. More than likely, he wanted the beagle to search for narcotics. Whatever. She didn't have any drugs in her house beyond ibuprofen and prenatal vitamins. Let him look to his heart's content.

Until he'd found the bags stashed in her van, the possibility that someone would hide them there had never crossed her mind. However, she didn't have a garage, so she parked her vehicle in front of her house. Anyone could've accessed it.

Right? Her home was different. It was a safe place. Her solace. Nobody would put drugs there for safekeeping.

Bennett slid from the driver's seat and released Spike while Naomi exited the vehicle. The contractions had stopped, but her exhaustion was tenfold from before the shootout at Peter's ranch.

She exhaled in relief at finally being home. Might as well enjoy the freedom until Detective Ford arrested her. As Naomi strode toward the front door, the baby resumed his ninja moves. She chuckled, relishing how it grounded her.

Naomi placed her hand over her son's tiny foot, which was still kicking. *Thank you, Lord, for this beautiful reminder of Your presence in my life.*

Bennett and Spike caught up with her. "Are you okay?"

"Yes, little man was on the move again."

"Good to hear." Bennett offered her a hand as she stepped onto the sidewalk from the parking lot.

To an outsider, the duo might appear protective. Instead, she recognized Bennett's motives for keeping her close. Sadness hovered like a fog. How could he think she'd kill Peter and the others? Her eyes welled with tears. She blinked them away, unwilling to show Detective Ford anything but quiet calmness. She was tired and her emotions were raw, balancing on the edge. The last thing she needed was to come apart at the seams in front of the man determined to arrest her for a murder—strike that, *murders*—she hadn't committed.

Eager to get inside and take a relaxing bath before bed, Naomi walked faster. She started to insert her key into the lock when the door opened.

She turned and caught Bennett's eye.

"Step to the side." He moved an arm defensively in front of her in a sweeping motion, one hand brandishing his gun. "Wait here until I clear the apartment." His tone was barely a whisper, but it held a firmness that left no room for argument.

Naomi flattened herself against the stone wall exterior.

"Spike, stay. Guard." Bennett removed the leash.

Clearly oblivious that his slight stature intimidated no one, the little beagle maneuvered in front of her in a solid stance.

Naomi shifted, attempting to peer around Bennett, earning her a warning look. Too exhausted to outrun another shooter, she retreated to her original position. The maternal instinct to protect her unborn child prevailed, and she inhaled a fortifying breath for courage.

Bennett entered her apartment, leaving the door ajar.

She glanced down at Spike, his compassionate eyes meeting hers. "It won't take long," she whispered, speaking more to herself than the dog. With two bedrooms and one bathroom, her cozy townhome was far from extravagant.

Bennett returned within minutes, holstering his gun, and snapped on Spike's leash. The look on his face compelled her to push past him.

Naomi stepped over the threshold and gasped at the destruction. With her hand over her mouth, containing the cry that threatened to escape, she slowly walked through her home.

The once lovely burgundy faux leather couch she and Ted had saved up to buy sat maliciously gutted. Slash marks ravaged the fabric and stuffing spewed from the inflicted wounds. She pivoted toward the bookcase where the mess continued with her belongings haplessly strewn across the carpet.

Pages from her favorite leather-bound classic books littered the floor and coffee table. The only framed picture she'd kept of her and Ted lay amid the shards of glass. The broken image contrasted Naomi's dreams of a happy family with their failed marriage. Her throat constricted as she knelt.

"No." Bennett's command and his hand on her arm halted Naomi in place.

Empathy filled his light brown eyes.

"You can't touch anything until the evidence technicians have documented the scene."

Naomi averted her gaze, everything within her aching physically and emotionally. Before she could stop it, the tears welled again, filling her eyes and blurring her vision. Bennett helped her to stand, supporting her lower back with one hand, and offered a light squeeze of her arm. Though she would normally resist his touch, her resolve had fled, leaving her vulnerable.

"I've called for assistance." His response offered no comfort.

Great, more cops. "My life is falling apart, and I don't understand why. What did I do to deserve this? Why now?" The questions tumbled out like the tears streaming down her face.

Naomi didn't look at Bennett. She also didn't withdraw from his touch, but she was grateful he didn't pull her into an embrace. The slight distancing helped her to remember their roles.

They weren't friends.

She walked to the bedrooms, where the destruction continued. Her heart dropped to the floor at the sight of her baby's crib shattered, his nursery destroyed. Naomi gasped and leaned against the door.

"It'll be okay," Bennett said, coming up behind her.

"How is it going to be okay?" she snapped, swiping the moisture from her face.

If she wasn't mistaken, Bennett seemed to wince at her reproach.

She didn't have the luxury of falling apart. Not now. There was no one to help her or lean on. Her baby shifted. He was all that mattered. This was just stuff. Naomi lifted her chin in a quiet resolve to fight, if not for herself, for her unborn son.

"It's not safe for you to stay here." He released his hold. "I'll help you gather whatever you need for a couple of days' stay."

"And where am I supposed to go?" She planted her fists on her hips. "It's not like I can sleep in my van."

"I live about twenty minutes from here." Bennett hoisted Spike into his arms. "You're welcome to stay with me."

Naomi shook her head. "No way."

"I realize it's a little unorthodox. However, I have a spare room."

"I'll be fine." She crossed her arms.

"Let me word this another way. You're still my prime suspect, like it or not—"

"As though I get an opinion?" It wasn't fair to unleash her emotions on Bennett, but he was the closest recipient. Even the sweet little beagle in his arms didn't prevent her from targeting him with her frustration.

"Of course you do." Bennett stroked the dog's fur. "Until I have more information on the drugs and the most recent events from tonight, I can't let you out of my sight. The offer to stay with me remains. If not, your alternative is for me to book you into the county jail."

Naomi gaped. Surely, he was joking. "On what charges?" She immediately regretted the question.

"Possession with intent to distribute, for starters." He answered matter-of-factly, like a glass of cold water in her face. "I don't want to do that, Naomi. But whoever did this—" he swept his arm wide as if reinforcing his point "—might not stop. Prison is full of criminals willing to kill for money. If they get wind you're incarcerated…"

Naomi swallowed hard. "Why would someone want me dead?"

"Good question."

A knock sounded. "Naomi?"

Naomi jerked upright, recognizing Addy's voice. Bennett stood with gun in hand. "It's Addy," she whispered. "The one who has the competitive tour company. Coming," she called, then swiped at her eyes and hurried to the stairs.

Addy stood in the living room, eyes wide. "What happened?"

"Someone broke into my home."

Bennett quickly descended behind her, gun poised.

Addy gasped.

"He's a cop," Naomi explained.

"Oh." Addy visibly relaxed. "I stopped by to bring you this."

She passed Naomi a stack of fliers. "I'm starting hiking tours and thought you could give them to your customers."

"Sure," Naomi said absently.

"This is an active scene, you'll have to leave," Bennett replied.

Addy crossed her arms. "You're a real charmer." She addressed Naomi. "Maybe you should go somewhere safe. Whoever did this—" she gestured toward the destroyed room "—might return."

Bennett stared at Addy. "Would you know anything about who that person might be?"

"Of course not! Probably one of her husband's deadbeat friends," Addy snapped.

"What did you know about Ted?" Bennett asked.

"Nothing more than he was a loser who should've helped his wife instead of abandoning her."

Naomi gaped at Addy. She'd never spoken about Ted that way before. Instead of feeling protected, the comment made her feel vulnerable.

"Shouldn't you be asking for backup or collecting evidence instead of interrogating an innocent citizen like me?" Addy challenged.

"I haven't interrogated you, ma'am," Bennett's eyes narrowed. "Perhaps we should start there."

"Thanks for stopping by, Addy." Naomi inserted herself. "I'll add these to my handout packet and send you any referrals."

"You're too close to your delivery date. You shouldn't be working this late into your pregnancy, anyway. Get some rest." Addy held Bennett's gaze for several seconds. "Let me know if you need anything." She spun on her heel and stomped away.

Bennett moved to the door, apparently confirming Addy had departed. "That's your friend?"

"She's nice when you get to know her."

He snorted, closing the door.

"Let me get my stuff together." Naomi moved past him and gathered an overnight bag, tossing in essentials, a couple of changes of clothes and a second pair of shoes.

She returned to where Bennett and Spike searched the room. "Looking for drugs?" The inquiry came out a little snarkier than she'd intended, but her politeness had evaporated.

"Yes." His quick reply should've shocked Naomi, but it didn't.

"Find any?"

"No."

"I could've told you that, but I'm glad you figured it out on your own." Naomi slung the bag over her shoulder.

"Until we're able to verify your alibi, you must remain close to me."

"You've made that clear." She softened her response while maintaining her distance. Better to be in his care than alone when whoever had destroyed her apartment returned. The men at Peter's ranch didn't believe her when she'd proclaimed no knowledge of the drugs. They would invoke whatever means necessary to threaten her. Naomi shivered at the implications. When she confessed the police had the drugs, what would they do then?

Why had someone targeted her? Were they using her van to mule? She'd read about criminals choosing an unsuspecting person, usually a teenager or a woman, and planting drugs on them.

Even if Bennett accepted Naomi wasn't involved, it didn't help her with the murder charges. How could he possibly suspect her of being a murderer? It was ludicrous.

"Do you need anything else?" Bennett glanced around the room.

"Proof I'm not a drug-dealing serial killer?" She made no effort to hide her sarcastic response. If Naomi failed to prove her innocence, her life would take a horrible turn of events.

* * *

Two hours later, Naomi clung to her backpack for dear life, treating the bag like a security blanket. Bennett had insisted on dropping off the drugs at the Denver Police Department before they drove to his downtown condo. That took longer than she'd expected, but waiting for him to finish processing the evidence gave her time to reschedule her tours with Addy, who was all too willing to take the extra business. Most of her customers were gracious, but the few that weren't stressed out Naomi. Still, she was grateful for Addy's help in the last-minute situation.

The burdens clung to her like a stone-filled sack. Losing Ted months prior had destroyed her dreams of a loving marriage. Now, she faced the loss of their business. Everything was being stripped from her, tearing at her heart one piece at a time.

"Coming?" Bennett called, jolting her from her thoughts.

Naomi hurried to catch up to him and Spike while surveying the high-rise building. Bennett held the glass entry door open, and they walked into the foyer, which was decorated in minimalist fashion. They rode the elevator to the eleventh floor, then exited and strolled down the long hallway. How did Bennett afford to live in a place like this? She shoved away the thoughts. What business was that of hers?

"Bennett, I appreciate this."

"No problem." He smiled, and unless Naomi was mistaken, it seemed genuine.

Spike trotted ahead as much as his long leash allowed. He rounded the corner and paused beside a door. Bennett inserted his key and pushed open the door, allowing Naomi to enter first. She stepped over the threshold, and he released Spike from his leash. The dog gave a thorough shake of his fur and strolled past her, obviously comfortable in his surroundings.

The open floor plan with a kitchen to her right and living area to the left was decorated in modest, neutral colors. A cozy dining space with a rectangular table divided the two rooms.

The powerful aroma of teakwood filled her senses, and she fought not to wrinkle her nose at the smell. She spotted the plug-in diffuser in the hallway.

As though sensing her thoughts, Bennett explained, "The lady at the store recommended this scent, and I haven't gotten used to it."

"It's got a strong masculine undertone," Naomi replied, sounding like a salesperson.

"That's one way to put it." He chuckled and hung Spike's leash on a small hook by the door. "Let me show you to your room."

Naomi trailed mutely behind him down a short hallway, her gaze roving for any inside information on Bennett Ford. No personal decor covered the walls, adding to her curiosity.

He gestured toward an open door, revealing a bathroom on one side and a bedroom on the other. A white wedding ring quilt covered the queen-sized bed, and the only other piece of furniture was a side table and lamp. "Make yourself comfortable."

She entered the space, instantly liking it. "Do you treat all your prisoners this nicely?"

"You're my first, to be fair," he teased.

"Thank you for giving me a place to stay that didn't involve orange jumpsuits."

"I'll let you get some rest."

"I wish I could." Naomi set her bag on the floor beside the bed. "Considering everything that's happened tonight, you'd think I'd pass out cold. But my mind won't stop racing. There's no way I can fall asleep right now." Her stomach rumbled, and she averted her eyes, cheeks warming with embarrassment. Food hadn't been on her mind, but apparently little man had other ideas.

Bennett's eyes widened. "I didn't even consider that you'd be hungry. It's close to midnight, but you must be starving. Is there anything you'd like? I could whip up something." Bennett turned toward the hallway. "I'm not home much, so it's hard to say what's in my fridge, but we'll figure it out."

"I am a little hungry." She shrugged. The incredible urge for chocolate cereal made her mouth water. No way was she asking for that. But once the thought entered her mind, it took on a life of its own. The craving was strong. Little man always got his way. "Whatever you want to do is fine. I'm not picky. Would you mind if I freshened up first?"

"Sure." Bennett tilted his head. "I'll put together something to eat."

"Thanks."

He blocked the doorway. "My experience with pregnant women is limited. Do you have any cravings?"

Naomi shifted from one foot to the other. "I do, but it's embarrassing."

"Why?" Bennett leaned back, crossing his muscular arms over his chest. "I don't have pickles, but there might be ice cream."

She laughed. "Um, no. Neither of those. I kind of crave… cereal."

"Like granola, shredded wheat?"

"Nothing healthy." She rubbed her belly, making circles with her hands. "He likes…chocolate puffs."

Bennett grinned. "Now that's a craving I can get on board with." He spun on his heel and hurried down the hallway.

Naomi stayed planted, surveying the space. The slam of a cabinet carried to her, and Bennett returned, carrying a box of her favorite breakfast cereal. "Like this?"

She stared, and it took all her self-control not to rip the box out of his hands. She envisioned herself tearing into the packaging and shoveling handfuls of the chocolaty delights into her mouth. "Yes," she chuckled, trying to maintain control. He grinned and turned back toward the kitchen.

Naomi hurried to the bathroom with her bag and closed the door.

When she emerged, the scent of bacon and toast filled the air, drawing Naomi to the kitchen. Bennett cut a sandwich in half. "BLTs with a side of cereal?"

"That sounds amazing." She grinned. "How can I help?"

"Grab the cereal and milk." Bennett gestured to the end of the counter. He carried the sandwiches on plates, placing them in front of two of the dining room chairs.

Naomi wasted no time sitting down and fixing a bowl of cereal.

After several satisfying bites, she reached for the BLT. Naomi bit into the sandwich, relishing the perfect blend of bacon, lettuce and tomato. They ate in silence and when she'd cleaned her bowl and plate, Naomi wiped her mouth. "I was hungrier than I thought. I inhaled that."

"Me too." Bennett leaned back. "Is great taste in cereal the only craving you've had?"

"No." Naomi picked at a piece of lettuce on her plate. "At first, I wanted baked potatoes, which is comical, considering I don't like them."

"I'll try not to hold that against you," Bennett teased.

She laughed. "I do like French fries."

"Well, it's a start." His conversational tone didn't match the tension evident in his posture.

Naomi couldn't help but notice Bennett's handsomeness. His blond hair reminded her of a model's, perfectly styled with that just-out-of-bed look that only attractive men could pull off. His light brown eyes held a hardness that spoke of experience and pain, but beyond that, laugh lines testified of better days when he must've smiled a lot. She wondered what had taken those away. She understood experiences that wounded a soul to the point of eliminating joy.

"After the great potato aversion, what happened?" He reengaged her in the discussion.

"That only lasted for the first month, then in the past six

weeks, all I want is chocolate puff cereal." She groaned. "Not exactly low-calorie nutrition."

"I'm far from judgmental regarding nutritional food. Cops learn to live on whatever is available when we have time to eat."

Bennett's financial status lingered in her mind. Who was she dealing with? "I apologize, but I have to ask something."

"Shoot."

"This is none of my business, but how do you afford to live in a downtown Denver condo this nice?" Her gaze roved the space.

"Beg your pardon?" His quizzical frown conveyed disapproval.

Naomi's ears warmed, but after all she'd endured, her politeness waned. "I haven't a clue what a cop's salary is, but it can't be enough to afford a place so nice. Not in this area." She fixed her gaze on Bennett, unwilling to relent in her challenge.

"Fair enough." Bennett leaned back in his chair. "It belonged to my grandmother in the days before this became the yuppie hot spot."

Relief coursed through her. "I apologize for the invasive question."

"You shouldn't. I'm a skeptic at heart, so I appreciate your willingness to call me out on anything you see as questionable." Sincerity hung in his features.

"Thank you." A subtle reminder of their roles sobered Naomi. "Did you always want to be a police officer?" She caught herself. "Sorry—detective."

"Yeah, pretty much." He sat up straighter and took a sip from his water glass. "My uncle was a DPD officer for over thirty years. In fact, I'm named after him."

"That's kind of cool." She tilted her head, silently pondering what her little boy would want to do when he grew up.

"I always looked up to him. He's a great guy."

Present tense meant the man was alive. Unexpectedly, Naomi's throat tightened with emotion. All she had left was her brother, whom she barely saw. She studied her belly a little too hard, focused on the T-shirt fabric.

Spike trotted out from the kitchen and paused beside her, allowing Naomi to run her fingers through his velvety fur. Strange, even after he'd found drugs in her vehicle, he didn't hold a grudge. If only humans were the same. "He's sweet."

At her declaration, Spike licked her hand and offered her a compassionate gaze before moving to a round dog bed near the sofa.

"He's an exceptional partner."

"Evan and I spoiled our family dog, Rusty. We always snuck him dinner treats." Naomi sighed. "Daddy would pretend to admonish us, but he was just as bad. Mama used to wag her finger, but then we'd catch her fixing Rusty his own plate of leftovers when she thought no one was looking."

Bennett grinned. "What kind of dog?"

"A purebred mutt." She smiled at the memories. "He had the fur of a golden retriever but the coloring of a black Lab. And, if you can picture this, the body of a Great Dane."

As she'd expected, Bennett's eyes widened.

"Right?" Naomi chuckled. "He was the gentlest creature. We had him for over fifteen years before he passed away. That hit us all hard. Rusty wasn't just a dog, he was a part of our family."

Bennett nodded, glancing at Spike. "I get that. Did you and Ted have dogs?"

"No, we worked long hours and agreed it wouldn't be fair to the animal." Fond memories of her deceased husband returned. "In our dating years, we hiked a lot." She glanced down at her belly. "I'm sure that's hard to picture given my current state."

"Not really. I can see you being outdoorsy."

"I love it."

He shifted forward, placing his elbows on his knees. "I'm not in the practice of speaking ill of the dead, but I'd like to ask you about Ted."

"Okay." Naomi hadn't missed the way his disposition had softened toward her. His emotional distance remained, but his tone was less accusatory and more inquisitive.

"Tell me about your marriage?"

She cringed. Of all the topics on the planet, talking about her failed relationship was the last on her list. Naomi hoped to divert. "We had our trials like most folks." She focused too hard on the wilting piece of lettuce on her plate, wishing she had more to eat to avoid the discussion.

"Were there any extenuating circumstances, especially toward the end?"

"You mean was my husband cheating on me? Or hurting me?"

"Yes, but also about Ted's behavior. Addy didn't seem to hold him in high regard."

Naomi considered his question. "Things were good in the beginning. We had fun together. He was my best friend and greatest confidant. I trusted him more than I'd ever depended on anyone before."

Her heart constricted at the memories of Ted's kindness and tenderness. But she couldn't ignore the painful memories of how he'd transformed toward the end.

"What changed?" Bennett probed, no doubt able to read her expression.

"It was like he had a complete personality exchange. Where he'd been thoughtful, he became distant and elusive. He quit holding my hand, something I cherished, like touching me repulsed him."

"Was the baby planned?" Bennett's cheeks reddened. "I'm sorry. I don't mean to—"

"As much as any baby, I suppose. He was a welcome surprise, but we weren't actively trying to have a child." She felt her own cheeks warm and averted her gaze. "We'd talked about having a family in the beginning. I hoped Ted would revert to those kinder years when I told him we were expecting."

"Did he?"

"At first, Ted was involved and excited, but money was a constant stressor. We had steady tours, which kept our heads above the financial waves, but he worried about the additional costs the baby brought to our lives. I reminded him that our trust wasn't in anything other than God. Ted wasn't a man of faith." She didn't add how he'd mocked her beliefs as flimsy and childish.

"Financial stress is common in young marriages." He tapped his fingers against his water glass. "Can't speak from personal experience, but that's what I've heard."

Naomi jumped on the opportunity to divert the discussion. "Never married or come close?"

"Close." Bennett's jaw hardened. "Dodged a fatal bullet there." She didn't have long to ponder because Bennett returned to interrogating her. "How did Ted handle the financial worries?"

"He started coming home late, if he bothered to at all, and making ridiculous excuses."

"You questioned his behavior?"

"At first, but once he moved out, I gave up. And then…he was gone." Naomi pushed back from the table and rose, collecting the dishes.

The confession solidified what Bennett already knew from his research into Naomi's life. "Leave it. I'll do them."

"Thank you. I'm tired. I'd like to go to bed."

"Absolutely." His eyes held a tenderness. "If you need anything, holler at me."

"Thanks." Naomi headed to the spare bedroom without looking back. The depressing past and pressure of the present hung heavy on her shoulders with an unbearable weight. Worse, her confusing emotions about Bennett intermingled with the mess. His kindness refreshed her heart after the desert dry loneliness she'd experienced. However, she reminded herself, it didn't negate his mission to arrest her for a crime she hadn't committed.

Naomi couldn't risk losing focus. Her life was on the line. Falling for someone like Bennett wasn't feasible, now or in the future.

And none of it would keep her out of prison.

SIX

After cleaning the kitchen, Bennett moved to the sofa, considering all that Naomi had shared. He studied her behavior as much as her words, and she didn't bear the usual evidence of a liar. She spoke with confidence and a certain grace. However, many psychopaths used their manipulative and charismatic personalities to lure their victims to their deaths.

She'd held his gaze, unrelenting. Not in defiance, more with a calm assurance. Nothing about her demeanor conveyed deception. But he wouldn't relax his suspicious nature until Isla had confirmed or destroyed her alibi.

Naomi had looked exhausted, and once more, the twinge of sympathy for the mother-to-be battled with his cynical views. She'd get plenty of rest in prison. Still, he was at the point of deciding whether to arrest her or let her go. For now. He knew where to find her, and she hardly posed a flight risk. Her explanation was plausible. Could Naomi be innocent of the drugs and the murders? But if she wasn't the RMK, who was?

A text from Isla chimed on his phone. Still up?

He quickly dialed, and she answered on the first ring. "You're working late."

"I figured you'd want an update ASAP."

"I do, thanks."

Naomi approached, wearing a pensive expression.

Bennett spoke into the phone. "Isla, can you hold one second?"

"No problem."

He pressed the cell against his chest. "Everything okay?"

"I'm sorry, I just remembered something." Naomi stood clinging to her small cosmetic bag. "I hate to ask this, but I have an OB appointment tomorrow morning. I'm so close to my due date, and after the hospital visit today, I'd really like to see my doctor."

"Uh, sure." Bennett processed the request, realizing the implications. "What time?"

"Ten forty-five in Littleton." Naomi referred to the suburb south of Denver.

"Sounds good."

"Thank you." Relief swept over her face.

She must have a million things to think about. Taking her to the doctor wasn't a big deal. Plus, it kept her near him, and he wouldn't have to worry about her trying to break into her van.

"Good night." She turned and headed for the bedroom, closing the door with a soft click.

Not that Naomi couldn't overhear his discussion, but he preferred to talk to his teammate privately. Placing the phone against his ear, he said, "Sorry about that, Isla. What do you know?"

"First, I got nothing on the hospital security footage. The man skillfully eluded the cameras."

"Great. That means he had knowledge of their location."

"Exactly."

Bill Nolice's cheerful face bounced to the forefront of Bennett's mind. "Dig into the security guard, Bill Nolice. He watched Spike for me when Naomi was admitted to the hospital."

"Will do." Isla continued. "Second, Naomi's alibi checks out with the hospice unit time sheet records. I also spoke to the nurse she mentioned, Yvette Jacobsen. She corroborated Naomi's claim that she was working at midnight."

"The same time the murders occurred ten years ago," Bennett concluded.

"Yep." Typing on Isla's end filtered through the line. "There's more. Naomi's tour bus records substantiate she was driving during the most recent murders of Peter Windham and Henry Mulder."

The sense of relief shocked Bennett, and for the first time since he'd confronted Naomi, he could breathe. "That's great news."

"Yeah, just one thing that struck me as strange. I contacted random passengers from Naomi's rosters to verify they rode with her on the scheduled days and times. Of course, I provided my creds right off the bat." Isla referenced her professional credentials as a member of the MCK9 team. "One woman felt compelled to reiterate how sweet Naomi was."

"Why was that strange?" Bennett asked.

"Just a feeling, ya know?" Isla paused. "She tried too hard to convince me of Naomi's innocence."

"Did you tell her why you were calling?"

"Of course not. But she made the law enforcement connection, and I'm telling you it was strange."

"What's her name?"

"Hazel Houston."

Bennett snorted. "Sounds like a made-up name."

"It is. Already ran a background and came up blank."

"So, why use a fake name and proclaim Naomi's innocence?"

"The line is disconnected, too, so I can't follow up," Isla said. "Also pulled Adeline Everett. She has a tour bus business that offers the same features as Naomi, including nature hikes coming in the summer. She's clean, other than a few parking tickets."

"Okay, thanks," Bennett replied. "Have you notified the team?"

"Was just about to."

"Let's do a quick group call. I have updates, too."

"I'll set it up and send the video conference link."

"Thanks." He'd never spoken truer words. He hadn't dined with a killer after all.

The link popped up on his phone, and Bennett connected with the team. Not surprisingly, the rest of them were also still awake and working. "Sorry for the late-night check-in," Bennett began.

"Justice never sleeps," Elk Valley PD Officer Ashley Hanson replied, appearing wide awake. A benefit no doubt of being the youngest member.

"Exactly." Bennett leaned back. "So, we have an update." He launched into an explanation of the events at Peter's ranch, the break-in at Naomi's apartment and the attack at the hospital.

"I've confirmed Naomi isn't our killer," Isla added, pulling back her long brown hair with one hand. "Her alibis check out for the past murders and present kills."

"Wow." Task force leader Chase Rawlston leaned closer, revealing shadows on his face that spoke of worry and the weight of leading the team.

"I dropped off the drug bags at DPD and requested a rush for fingerprint and DNA testing," Bennett advised. "We'll have data soon."

"Does someone owe you big?" Teasing flickered in Idaho Deputy Selena Smith's green eyes and a grin played on her lips.

"Something like that." Bennett chuckled. "Never underestimate the power of connections."

"True." New Mexico Bureau FBI agent Kyle West joined the discussion.

Bennett had heard people describe him as intense with his dark hair and eyes, but Bennett failed to see him that way.

"Until we have the results from the bags, we cannot completely discount Naomi's involvement with the drugs," Chase reminded the group. "And just because she wasn't the one who pulled the trigger, it doesn't exclude her from being involved with the RMK."

"Everyone has enemies, even if they're unaware," Bennett replied. Though he wanted to argue, Chase's comment was a reality check for him. He doubted Naomi was the RMK, but he'd been wrong before in trusting a woman he shouldn't. He shifted his focus on the commander and told himself to remain professional and impartial. "Any word on Cowgirl?"

"Not a thing," Isla responded with a long exhale. No wonder she'd cut Bennett off earlier. She was juggling a hundred different things at the same time.

"If she was dognapped, did the thief have great coordination skills?" Elk Valley PD Officer Rocco Manelli strode closer, revealing his tall, slender frame.

"Yep," Utah Highway Patrol State Trooper Hannah Scott replied while simultaneously whipping her long red hair into a clip.

"She'll attract attention in town," Bennett said.

"Her markings will help," Selena agreed. "Though Labradoodles are a common breed, the telltale dark brown splotch on her right ear gives us a unique feature to give the public."

"Liana has posters around town." US Marshal Meadow Ames sat close to her camera, filling the frame with her contrasting dark hair and green eyes. "And she's blasting social media with information and pictures of Cowgirl, too."

"We have SAR dogs," Bennett said, referring to the team's dedicated search and rescue K-9s.

"We're doing everything to find her," Chase assured them.

Bennett clamped his mouth shut. Doubtful the boss appreciated his implication that he'd not allocated resources adequately.

"I've authorized Bennett to hold off on citing Naomi for drug possession and arresting her until we get the results from the fentanyl bags," Chase advised, turning the discussion back to Naomi.

Bennett got to his feet and glanced at the spare room where Naomi roomed. The door was closed, but he lowered his voice and moved to the furthest end of the living room. "I could be wrong, but I don't think Naomi's involved with this. Unless she's one exceptional actress, she's shaken up by the cascading events. I propose we go over the suspects, those with motives, enemies, etcetera, and expand our search."

"Agreed. However, in the meantime, I'd like to see what results we get with the fingerprint analysis," Chase replied. "Everyone, get a good night's rest and let's do a briefing tomorrow evening." With that, the team ended the call.

Bennett dropped onto the recliner and leaned forward, head in his hands. He prayed silently for wisdom to view Naomi through the eyes of an investigator. If Delaney had taught him anything, it was that the best deceptive wolves dressed in convincing sheep's clothing. A nudge to his hand reverted his attention to where Spike sat. Bennett stroked the dog's fur. "I wish you talked."

Spike gave a soft sigh.

"What do you think?" Bennett glanced toward the hallway. He recalled the conversation and Naomi's request to drive her to the doctor. Unsure what that entailed, a sudden rush of nerves got a hold of him. Recalling how the hospital personnel treated him as though he was the father-to-be, he groaned. *Ugh.*

Bennett leaned his head against the sofa cushions, still stroking Spike, who offered no wisdom. However, the beagle's interactions with Naomi said a lot. He was no Belgian Malinois, like Selena's K-9, Scout. Spike didn't have the intimidation factor, but he had good dog sense about people. He'd accepted Naomi from the start, separating her from the drugs. Bennett considered his training, reminding himself that psychopaths were skilled at manipulation. He met Spike's soulful gaze.

Dogs weren't easily fooled. Wouldn't Spike see through her lies? He'd never liked Delaney. That should've been a bright red flag from the start.

If he was wrong, he'd provided Naomi every opportunity to finish him in the middle of the night. Had he invited a serial killer to sleep under his roof?

Bennett jerked upright from his deep sleep, instinctively snagging his duty weapon and aiming it at his locked bedroom door. Spike sat up beside him with an annoyed expression. He yawned with an accompanying squeak as the phone rang a second time. Bennett lowered the gun and glanced at the cell, shaking his head to awaken himself.

He reached for the device and hurriedly swiped the screen after seeing DPD crime lab technician Eduardo Gomez's contact information.

"Hey, Eduardo," he croaked, hating the way his voice confirmed he'd just woken up.

"Rise and shine, Clementine." Eduardo chuckled.

"It was a late night." Bennett scrubbed a hand across his face.

"Not sure what you're hoping for on the outcome, but I got a fingerprint match on the bags of fentanyl."

That got Bennett's full attention. "And?"

"Ted Cavanaugh, based off a concealed carry permit application."

"No kidding," Bennett mumbled under his breath.

"Yep."

"Outstanding work. Thanks again for the rush."

"No problem, but this makes us even, right?"

"Right." Bennett chuckled.

"Cool. Later." Eduardo disconnected.

The running joke between him and Eduardo about who owed who never ended. But this was important, and he'd not waste the request on anything trivial. Bennett understood it was a big ask to rush the results, and he appreciated Eduardo's friendship.

The drug case added to Bennett's already full investigative

plate of apprehending the RMK. But he had to follow every lead, and if Naomi was connected to the drugs, he'd do whatever it took, even if it meant arresting her. Thanks to Eduardo's information, he wouldn't have to do that today.

Bennett threw off the blankets and stepped into a pair of running pants and shoes, then leashed Spike. He unlocked his door, feeling silly for his overreaction the prior night, and tugged it open. After scribbling a message on a sticky note to Naomi, advising he'd taken Spike out for a walk, he activated the motion sensor camera on his doorbell. Then they exited the condo, took the stairs to incorporate extra exercise, and pushed through the stairwell door to the empty foyer.

They strolled in front of the condo's entrance. While Spike sniffed and did his business, Bennett monitored his door video. Once Spike finished, they quickly hurried back.

Sounds from inside Naomi's room indicated she was awake. He sent a quick group text to the team, advising them of the findings and notifying them Eduardo would forward the report to Isla.

His phone lit up with their responses and Chase's order for a short video conference in ten minutes.

Bennett freshened up and rushed to the kitchen for a bottled water, prepared to join the chat three minutes prior to the scheduled time when Naomi emerged from her room.

"Good morning," Bennett said.

"Mornin'." Her bedraggled hair and rumpled, oversized T-shirt enhanced her adorableness.

Bennett blinked. What was wrong with him? "Uh, I have a task force meeting shortly."

"I'll get ready." Naomi turned and headed for the bathroom.

In the excitement of Eduardo's call, Bennett had forgotten about the OB appointment. Visions of sitting in a waiting room packed with pregnant women collided into him.

Where are you? Isla's text bounced over the chiming phone and redirected his attention.

Great.

He quickly signed into the video conference. "Good morning. Sorry I'm late."

The comment earned him quizzical looks from his teammates.

"Why are you so cheerful?" Hannah groused.

"Eduardo's results point to Ted Cavanaugh?" Rocco asked. "That's a plot twist."

Bennett nodded. "It's clear Naomi's husband was responsible for the drugs. And I believe the thugs who attacked us at Windham Ranch were in cahoots with him."

"Why wait to confiscate them? Were they aware Cavanaugh hid the drugs in her van?" Selena asked. "And how does that fit with the murder of Peter Windham?"

"Maybe it doesn't," Hannah said. "Could be two different and unrelated cases."

"All excellent discussion," Chase said. "But for this call, let's focus on the RMK investigation. Review the victims again, searching specifically for any enemies. There must be a connection tying them together."

"We already had that with Naomi," Rocco added. "She was the victim of a prank they'd played on her. She *is* the common denominator."

"There's obviously more to the story," Hannah said. "We need to find it."

"Peter Windham had no enemies," Kyle reminded the group.

"Everyone's got enemies," Chase argued. "Old Peter just might not have known it."

"I agree. Naomi is still our link to the victims, and it's clear she remains in danger based on the attacks at the ranch and hospital," Selena said.

"But the evidence doesn't support her as the RMK," Bennett reiterated. "However, the fentanyl and her deceased husband's involvement might give us something. Doubtful the men who attacked her at the ranch chose that location by accident."

"Agreed," Ashley said. "Still, there are that many connections to Naomi without them tying into the murders. Elk Valley is the relative point, so the RMK lived there or nearby."

"The YRC is also a factor," Hannah said. "I'll dig into past memberships."

"Hmm, or rejected potential members," Ashley added.

"Definitely," Rocco said.

"Were there other young women that experienced what Naomi did?" Meadow asked.

"It's possible," Isla said. "They were quite the group."

"Good. Dig into anyone else who fits the profile," Chase advised.

"I'll take Spike back to the impound lot to scour Naomi's van in the daylight." Bennett hesitated, then said, "First, though, I, uh, have to take Naomi for her obstetrician appointment this morning."

His coworkers' expressions conveyed more than the accompanying quiet. If he didn't miss it or misjudge it, Ashley stifled a smirk.

"I'll keep her close until we get this figured out," Bennett continued, aware he had overjustified his actions. "Whoever is after her won't stop until they get what they want."

"True, and if they want those drugs, it'll get ugly when she can't produce them," Selena added. "Kyle and I are headed to the Windham murder site. If the thugs followed Naomi there, perhaps we'll find evidence tying them to the crimes."

"Keep us updated," Chase said.

"We'll also hunt through the evidence files," Kyle said. "Selena and I requested the lab results from both Windham and Mulder's crime scenes."

"Are there updates on Cowgirl?" Bennett glanced where Spike sat waiting for his breakfast.

"None," Chase replied.

A momentary silence conveyed the team's worry and sadness for Cowgirl's situation.

"I'll also send you lists of any recent murders in the surrounding states," Isla said.

"Yes, let's wrap this up," Chase inserted. "Search for links, connections and common or related repetitive things."

A collective response of "Roger that" and "Affirmative" sounded from each of the members before they disconnected. Relieved that Naomi was no longer a suspect warred with Bennett's uncomfortableness at having to accompany her to the appointment. But the beautiful, scared, pregnant woman needed someone to watch her back.

Bennett couldn't shake the question that remained. Who was the RMK?

By the time he'd finished putting away his laptop and walked out of his bedroom, Naomi was sitting on the sofa, scrolling on her phone. "Hey, I'm still working out a few details for my rescheduled tours. I called the dealership, and they'll repair the windows once the impound lot releases my van." She met his eyes with expectation and hope.

"We should be able to get that handled soon." Unless Spike found more drugs.

"Okay." She reverted her attention to her phone again. She'd tied her hair back into a loose ponytail with tendrils framing her face. If she wore makeup, it was lightly applied. Her long, dark lashes emphasized her hazel eyes. In the morning light, Bennett noticed they held splashes of deep green. Naomi was truly beautiful.

What? No. He shook off the thoughts with a grunt.

"Why are you looking at me like that? Is something wrong?"

"No, no. It's good. Fine. Everything is okay. In fact, I have good news. Your alibis checked out for the five murders. And you're no longer a suspect in the drug case."

"Really? Why?"

He couldn't share the confidential details of an ongoing investigation. He'd offer limited information. Strangely, at the moment, he didn't want to explain everything to her…at least, not yet. Though he wasn't sure why. He'd tell her more if the situation presented itself. "Evidence excludes you from the drugs I confiscated from your van, so I won't have to charge you with possession."

"That's fantastic news!" She pushed herself to her feet and walked to the kitchen. "I didn't want to eat breakfast without you. But little man is starving. I'm merely his transportation."

Bennett chuckled. *Stop it.* How could he feel so right around her while fully aware of his own emotional walls? Nothing could come from their interactions. "Does the name Hazel Houston mean anything to you?"

"No." Naomi shook her head. "Sounds like a movie star or singer. Why?"

"She's listed in your travel manifest and seemed compelled to proclaim your innocence."

"Hmm. Maybe we bonded during a trip? I talk to my customers a lot while we're driving. Though I don't remember her, maybe she remembers me? I am innocent, after all." She grinned.

"Right." He snorted. "How about if I whip up eggs?"

"Actually, if you don't mind, I'm craving cereal again. Little man pretty much wakes me with his menu requests." She flashed him a smile that nearly buckled his knees.

He needed coffee urgently, before he did something he'd regret.

"I suppose he gets the final say." Bennett hurried to gather bowls and spoons while Naomi pulled out the milk and cereal, placing them on the table.

"Yep, he runs my life and my schedule, along with my tours." She poured herself cereal and passed the box to him.

"I'm sorry about the customers you lost with all this."

"Me too, but most were understanding." She dipped her spoon into the bowl. "Honestly, this is the first day off I've had in eight months."

"In that case, I don't feel too bad." He crunched away at

the sugary treat. "What does it say about me that my grocery preferences are the same as a child?"

"No judgment here." Naomi winked good-naturedly.

"I'd like to run to the impound lot before we go to your appointment." A glance at the clock confirmed they had time.

"Works for me."

They finished breakfast and cleaned the dishes, moving around the condo in a comfortable synchronicity. He struggled with the strange connection they had, as though they'd always known one another. It was too easy being with Naomi.

Bennett realized how much he enjoyed it.

Spending time with Naomi was far too dangerous.

SEVEN

Naomi settled into the passenger seat in Bennett's pickup. After years of driving others around, she appreciated the ease of riding. Traffic was light due to the early morning hours, making for a short commute to the impound lot.

"Because of the recent evidence, I'd like to revisit the topic of your marriage," Bennett said, "since we never finished the discussion."

Naomi did a double take. "What're you talking about?"

He hesitated, as though debating what to tell her. Was he withholding information?

"If you've found something, I have a right to hear about it."

"Yes and no." He focused on the road.

"That's a cop out."

"But it's valid." Bennett shrugged. "Did Ted own a personal gun?"

The shift had Naomi lingering in order to traverse back to their early relationship years. "I think so. And that was a lousy way to dodge my question."

"I promise there's a connection to my incessant interrogations."

"In that case—" Naomi acquiesced "—he had a pistol before we were married. I wouldn't allow him to keep any weapons in our home." She tried to remember where Ted had put the gun. "Now that you mention it, I have no clue if or where he kept it."

"That's a long answer to a short question."

"I'm not trying to be difficult. It just didn't cross my mind. Why?"

"His fingerprints are on file with the state for a concealed carry permit."

Naomi shrugged. "Okay…"

"Ted's prints were on the bags of drugs I confiscated from your van."

She twisted to face him. Had she heard him correctly?

"As I explained before, I don't like speaking ill of the deceased," Bennett began. "However, it's the reason I have to ask you a lot of questions."

"I…" She hesitated, fidgeting with her tunic fabric. "He…" Why couldn't she get any words out that made sense? "Ted was dealing drugs?"

"Until I have more information, I can't answer that. His fingerprints were on the bags, which alludes to the possibility that he placed them in the fender liner prior to his death."

Naomi rubbed her temple. "It's too early in the morning to learn my deceased husband was a drug dealer."

"Was he a user?"

"Not that I am aware of. He was as straitlaced as they come." In the beginning. Except she couldn't deny how Ted's mannerisms had changed drastically from their dating days until his death. He'd started by evading her. Then he'd ignored her questions about his whereabouts, making ridiculous excuses for why he chose to sleep in the spare room. Until eventually, he stopped coming home all together.

"You're awfully quiet."

"Sharing this is humiliating."

"That's not my goal at all." Bennett reached over and gently squeezed her hand.

The kind gesture touched her heart.

"I need a better picture of your daily lives."

"I understand." Naomi considered her next words. She exhaled. Remembering Ted used to hurt. Now, it was like telling someone else's story. "He'd left me emotionally before his horrible accident. You're probably already aware he drained our bank accounts, leaving me penniless except for the tour bus business, which barely makes ends meet."

"What did he do with the money?"

"Not a clue." Would it make any difference? Doubtful, but the unknowns left worse images than hearing the truth.

"Was your brother aware of your marital issues?"

"I never saw the necessity of involving Evan. I keep to myself." With the loss of her parents, and the rare times she got to spend with Evan, loneliness had become a normal way of life.

"Did you know Ted's friends?"

"He didn't have many."

"So, you're not sure if Ted was involved with anyone shady or new?"

Naomi sighed, focusing out her window. "It would be easy to say yes, putting all the blame for the drugs you found on my tour bus on Ted."

"True."

"I'd prefer denying it all to preserve his memory, but truthfully, I don't know. He apparently lived another life in the last part of our marriage. I already explained how I'd hoped the baby would give Ted more of a stake in our life together. Instead, the news pushed him further away emotionally…physically." She didn't want to look at Bennett, so she kept her gaze on the landscape passing by. "My parents were happily married, so I had a good example. Not that I'm oblivious to the hardship of relationships or the fact that they take work. And at first, I figured that's all that was happening with him when he started coming home late and lying about where he'd been."

"What clued you into his deception?"

"Ted was no Jason Bourne." Naomi snorted, her ears warming at the unladylike sound. "He didn't have the greatest excuses. The lies I'd caught him in broke my heart, and each one separated us a little further apart."

"Did you call him out?"

Naomi winced. This is where he'd judge her for weakness because she'd not walked out on Ted. Compelled to justify her reasons, she said, "I believe in the sanctity of marriage. I took a vow before God, and that meant something to me."

"I understand."

"You think I'm naive for not leaving him." She lifted her chin, defensiveness rising.

"Not at all. If I ever got married, I'd want it to be forever."

At his heartfelt confession, Naomi's wariness deflated, and she turned to look at Bennett. Everything within her hollered to keep her distance and watch what she said, so he wouldn't use it against her. Yet something about him tore through her heart armor.

A part of Naomi trusted Bennett, which made no sense. Except she couldn't shake that phenomenon of comfort, as though she'd known him forever. And that was wrong on so many levels. Before today, Detective Bennett Ford had considered the possibility that she was a drug-dealing serial killer.

"He stopped loving me a long time ago." The words escaped before Naomi realized she'd spoken aloud. Still, it was the truth, not a ploy for sympathy, just the reality of her life. "I tried everything to save our marriage. Counseling. Praying harder." She glanced down at her belly. "Even hoped that this little blessing would change his heart and draw us together. Sounds ridiculous, but my heart was desperate."

"Not at all."

"Ted wasn't the same guy I'd married. He moved out a month before his death, claiming he needed space. I didn't argue, praying he'd return. He never did." Admitting the truth eased some of her stress. "He spent a lot of nights at our tour bus office, and we worked together. In fact, he was checking out locations for nature hikes when he died. We wanted to stay competitive by adding those options."

Bennett's gaze remained on the road ahead. Several long

beats passed before he said, "Naomi, what if Ted's death wasn't an accident?"

"Ted was a skilled hiker."

"Yet he fell down a steep cliff." A statement, not a question.

"Even professional outdoorsmen can't avoid accidents. It's not like someone ran him off the road." Naomi studied the handsome detective.

Silence hung between them. She appreciated that he didn't push her. Instead, he remained quiet, allowing Naomi to think.

Images of the past twenty-four hours slammed into her, along with the realization that Ted had hidden the drugs in the van. "Although, until yesterday, I accepted the coroner's report at face value."

"There are some twists in the narrative." Bennett pulled into the impound facility.

Naomi struggled to process all the information. Why would Ted put her and the baby at such risk?

Bennett showed his credentials to the officer working the gate, and they passed through, traveling to the far side of the lot.

When they neared the van, Naomi stared in disbelief at the mutilated vehicle. Surely the mass of metal Swiss cheese wasn't hers. The distinctive flower paint decoration and her business number said otherwise.

Bennett shut off the engine, but Naomi didn't wait for him. She threw open her door and got out of the truck, set on inspecting the damage.

Numerable bullet holes pierced the exterior, and all the windows were gone.

"What happened to my van?" Naomi cried.

Bennett moved to her side with Spike. "How did this happen?" His jaw tightened and his narrowed eyes spoke of confusion and fury at the sight. His reaction offered some comfort.

"How did they get in here?" Naomi surveyed the chain-link fence that surrounded the property.

Bennett withdrew his phone. "Give me a second."

She listened as he made a call.

"Deputy McClintock, this is Detective Ford. I'm here with Naomi Carr-Cavanaugh—the owner of the van—at the impound lot." A pause. "Yes, I'm confused how anyone got in here, let alone inflicted this much damage."

Naomi continued surveying the vehicle, remaining close enough to eavesdrop on the call.

"Um, no. The shooters had blasted out the back window and tires." Bennett ran a hand over his head, agitation clear in his expression. "No, ma'am. How long did it take to get it impounded?"

That got Naomi's attention, and she moved closer.

"Yes, I'd love to see pictures. Thank you." He disconnected and faced her. "Apparently, when Deputy McClintock arrived to get the van, it had already sustained this damage. She's texting photos for us to compare."

Within seconds Bennett's phone pinged, and he held it out, allowing Naomi to examine the pictures. True to the deputy's account, bullets pulverized her van prior to the impounding.

"Those goons watched us leave?" Naomi surmised, placing a hand over her mouth.

"That's what I'm thinking." Bennett sighed, pocketing the phone. "Deputy McClintock got called out to an incident on the highway after receiving orders to impound your van. She got there as soon as she could."

"Why didn't they send someone else?"

"Staffing is always an issue. Too many incidents, not enough responders. An impounded vehicle takes lower precedent over a vehicular accident. Worse, they're lengthy to process."

"Which provided the shooters plenty of uninterrupted time to destroy my van." Although Naomi understood the logic, she couldn't help but wonder what would've happened if the deputy had arrived sooner.

He moved closer, inspecting the damage. "These guys are bold."

Bennett's voice faded behind her as Naomi walked to the driver's side and peered through the shattered window. She had nothing left. Without the van, she couldn't conduct her business. "Oh God, what am I going to do?" She whispered the desperate prayer. Hopelessness weighed on her with such force she wanted to collapse.

The thugs who'd done this wouldn't accept her word, and she shuddered to think what they'd do to her.

She glanced at Bennett.

The handsome detective had worked hard to protect her, but one man against two or more crazed killers weren't great odds.

Another survey of her van confirmed Naomi's fear.

There wasn't a person in the world strong enough to save her. *God, I need You.*

Bennett raged at the sight, mentally berating himself for not ordering security at the ranch. He recalled the earlier conversation with Deputy McClintock. Her confusion about safeguarding the van in the impound lot made sense now. Why protect this mess?

The shooters had waited for them to leave, then returned to search for the drugs. The cowards probably assumed Bennett had called for backup. Whatever the reason, he sent a silent prayer of gratitude that Naomi hadn't been one of their casualties.

He approached her. "Deputy McClintock and her team collected ballistic evidence from the scene, and it's already on its way to my contact at DPD for processing." The words tasted like a betrayal. Platitudes weren't helpful.

She looked at him, face crumpling. Tears streamed down her cheeks, and helplessness consumed him.

"Why?" The single question carried with it the desperation of her heart and situation.

Against the voice in Bennett's head reminding him of their respective roles, he pulled Naomi's body, racked with sobs, into his arms. Even Spike moved closer to her. The beagle sensed her hurt and offered comfort. Bennett rubbed Naomi's back, unsure what to do. He feared for the baby. "Shh, Naomi, it'll be fine. Somehow. Focus on your son. Calm down for him."

She surprised him by releasing her hold and swiping at her face. "Right. I'm okay."

"Liar." His mouth quirked in a half smile.

"Guilty as charged, but I need to see the rest of the damage."

"Are you sure?"

"Yeah, no point in pretending it's not horrendous."

Together, they inspected the interior, where the destruction reminded him of Naomi's apartment—vicious and unrelenting.

Bennett led her away from the vehicle. "Naomi, I'd like Spike to inspect everything once more. I doubt we'll find anything." He jerked his chin toward the van. "They most likely didn't either. That kind of mutilation speaks to pure fury or a warning."

Her eyes widened.

He winced. "Sorry, I guess I should've phrased that better."

"I'd rather hear the ugly truth." She shook her head. "Ted must've used the van to hide drugs. How could I have been blind to his activities? Why would he put me and the baby in danger?"

"This is not your fault. You are not responsible for Ted's actions." The comment washed over Bennett. Was his callous skepticism a product of blaming himself for Delaney's deceit? He'd taken in the humiliation, accepting responsibility for her crimes. He was no more accountable for her decisions than Naomi was for Ted's.

She nodded, swiping again at her cheeks with a tissue she'd produced from her purse. Bennett squeezed her shoulder, resisting the urge to pull her close. It had felt so right to hold her, but that wasn't fair to her or him. He should've come alone. Still, this was a first for him.

His cell phone chimed with a text from Isla. The hospital

security footage wasn't altered by Bill Nolice. The perp just avoided cameras. Nolice's background is clean. Ex-military, awarded several medals.

He responded. Thanks.

The information didn't preclude Nolice from assisting the intruder in Naomi's room, but it didn't point to him as an accomplice.

Naomi's continuing sobs drew his attention. She fell apart, crying to the extent of full hiccups between her words. "He. Shouldn't. Have."

Bennett placed a hand on her shoulder. "Breathe. Calm down. Think of your baby."

Naomi inhaled, hiccupping.

"Good. Take deep breaths," he encouraged.

She exhaled and blew her nose on the tissue. "You're right." She hiccupped. "It's just…a van."

"We won't let them get away with it. Let's shift into offensive mode."

She tilted her head. "Now is not the time to play football."

The seriousness of her comment exploded a guffaw from him, which made her laugh. "No, I meant instead of us being on the defensive, taking the hits as they dish them, let's get ahead of them."

Their chuckling quieted, and he elaborated, "For all of this to happen six months after Ted's death raises questions." Bennett scoured his mind for information and landed on the possibility that Ted wasn't alone in the drug business.

"I'm not following you."

"What if one of your 'customers'—" Bennett made air quotes with his fingers "—hid the drugs?" Had someone followed Naomi, using her van to transport the drugs? Had Ted done that all along?

If Ted had an accomplice, it explained the time delay between his death and the arrival of the thugs at the ranch. However, it didn't expound on why.

"I suppose anything is possible."

"Let Spike and I search. Are you all right waiting here?"

She nodded and produced another tissue.

Bennett rushed to his truck, retrieved the stuffed taco, and placed it in his pocket. He knelt beside the beagle and used his voice inflection to inspire the dog. "Okay, Spike, ready to work?"

The beagle's white-tipped tail wagged excitedly.

"Let's find some cookies. Find the cookies!"

Spike took off toward the van, running to the full extension of his lead. Bennett trailed as the dog made his way, nose in full force. Spike aimed for the rear tires where the intruders had torn out some of the flooring.

He barked twice, paused and barked again, then lay down.

Bennett scanned the area with his flashlight, finding nothing. The alert meant Spike detected the scent of narcotics. Though none were currently present, the drugs left a lingering odor or residue. The location correlated to the hidden compartment under the van's rear fender well where he'd found the fentanyl inside the liner. Whoever was involved with Ted Cavanaugh assumed he'd placed the drugs there or had placed them there to retrieve later. Based on the destruction they'd left behind, they were resolute to hurt Naomi.

He glanced out the shattered window where she stood, head held high, exuding confidence and grace. In that moment, Bennett decided he'd do whatever it took to protect her and her baby. He wouldn't let her out of his sight until he found the villains responsible.

Bennett surveyed the area, then glanced at his watch. They had to get on the road if they planned to make Naomi's doctor appointment. Leading Spike from the van, Bennett walked to her.

"We'd better go."

She nodded, and he helped her into the truck before loading Spike.

A Douglas County Sheriff's cruiser pulled up beside his pickup.

"I'll be right back." Bennett walked to the patrol unit as the deputy exited.

"Again, Detective, I apologize for the miscommunication. I assumed you were aware of the damage."

"They returned after we'd left." He gestured to his truck. "We're late for an appointment. If you find anything that might help in the investigation, please contact me immediately."

"Understood."

"I appreciate it." Bennett strode to his pickup and slid behind the wheel. He texted the team with pictures of the van and a quick update, then started the engine and exited the property.

Once they were on the road, Naomi said, "Thank you for helping me to put things into perspective."

"How did I do that?"

"You reminded me of what's important. I must keep calm for the sake of my baby. The last thing I want is to spend another day at the hospital with Braxton-Hicks contractions." She leaned back in the seat. "The next time I show up there, it'll be to deliver."

"Sounds like a solid plan to me." Bennett reached over and squeezed her hand. "I am truly sorry for all you're going through."

"Thank you. Me too."

Bennett merged onto the highway.

"I'm baffled at the overkill damage to my van."

"Yeah." He gritted his teeth as images of what would've happened to Naomi if he hadn't been at Windham Ranch when the men showed up.

Both had their windows down, and a light breeze filtered through the cab.

Bennett traveled Santa Fe Drive, taking a route that paralleled Interstate 25, avoiding the rush hour traffic. They'd gone several miles when he noticed a large truck speeding from behind.

"Do not panic. We have unwanted company. Please scoot down as much as your seat belt allows." Then he shouted, "Spike, kennel!"

The dog disappeared into the steel box and a click sounded, confirming the automatic lock had fallen into place.

"What's going on?" Naomi twisted to look behind her.

"I'm not sure yet." Bennett's gaze bounced between the rearview mirror and the road ahead. "But I'm certain we don't want them getting too close to us."

A revving engine behind them nearly muted his statement. Bennett reached for his weapon, steadying the vehicle. There was no place to turn off the road that wouldn't put them at worse risk. He had to keep moving and get to highway C-470.

The truck sped up on Bennett's side.

He glanced at Naomi just as she cried, "Gun!"

"Stay down!" Bennett ducked and jerked the wheel.

His pickup slammed into the other vehicle.

Gunshots exploded through the cab, missing them while shattering Naomi's side mirror.

She squealed, covering her head with her arms.

Undeterred, their pursuers rammed into her door, attempting to force Bennett's truck into the heavy guardrail.

He fought to maintain control against the bullies. The cab filled with the grinding of metal on metal.

Finally, Bennett forced his way out of the battle, accelerating ahead. "Naomi, can you reach into the console? There's a lockbox. Enter the code four two zero five and get my backup weapon."

"Yes, I think so." She turned from her position on the floor. In an awkward twist, she retrieved the Sig Sauer. Naomi held out the pistol with both hands, clearly uncomfortable handling the gun.

"Tell me you've shot before." Even as Bennett spoke, he knew the response.

"No." She shook her head vehemently. "It's heavy."

"Two days ago, it would've thrilled me to hear that." Bennett groaned. "At the moment, I was hoping you'd say otherwise."

"I mean, I can try." She lifted the gun with both hands, whipping the barrel to face him.

He ducked. "Keep the weapon downward at all times unless you're firing it."

"Sorry." She winced, turning the gun downward, uncertainty still written on her face.

The truck drew closer again.

Bennett maneuvered his Silverado unsuccessfully to avoid the hit.

The shooters nudged his bumper, completing the tactical maneuver, sending Bennett's pickup fishtailing. He gripped the wheel, recovering quickly, and pulled out of the skid.

Naomi clenched the seat with both hands. "Is Spike safe back there?"

"Yes." Bennett didn't elaborate. The fully enclosed kennel secured Spike from the gunfire, and he prayed it would also protect him from the jostling.

Several vehicles approached in the oncoming lane.

Naomi screamed.

Gunshots erupted from the pursuer's passenger window as they sped past, nearly colliding head-on with a semi before swerving in front of Bennett.

The steering wheel tugged to the right. "They hit a tire!" Bennett slowed, still fighting for control.

Ahead, the shooters swerved all over the road, then turned off at the next exit, disappearing from sight.

EIGHT

"Is it over?" Naomi's fingers dug into the seat cushion, eyes squeezed shut.

"For now."

She opened her eyes and released her hold.

Bennett extended his hand, helping her get into her seat. "Are you okay?"

"Uh-huh." Honestly, her muscles were strained and aching. Her gaze roved the road, occupied with morning travelers. "If only they'd been there a little while ago," she mused.

"Yep, that's what scared them off."

The truck rode awkwardly and a *womp-womp* sound carried from the rear.

"What is that?"

"A flat tire courtesy of those creeps. Based on the way my gas gauge is looking, they also hit the fuel line, so I don't want to stop anywhere on this road." Bennett focused ahead.

Naomi glanced out the windshield, spotting several vehicles approaching from behind them and in the oncoming lane.

"Please use my phone and text my teammates, Selena Smith and Kyle West. Tell them where we are and ask them to meet us." He jerked his chin downward, where his cell peeked from his shirt pocket.

Naomi withdrew the device and held it out, allowing Bennett to hold his thumb over the reader to unlock it. Once the device came to life, she opened a new message.

"Tell them we have the partial Colorado license plate number of our assailants," Bennett instructed. "Advise 'K, seven, ten.' That's all I read off of it. We'll meet at the Linkhalter Steel parking lot just off Titan Road."

The truck's tire continued making the *womp-womp* sound.

"I need to pull over soon before I ruin the rim." Bennett pointed ahead, where Naomi spotted a large sign high above a warehouse building.

"Got it." She sent the message and within seconds received their chimed responses. "They're on their way," Naomi reported. "ETA ten minutes."

"Good. Hey, Spike, how're you doing?"

A sharp bark emitted from behind Naomi, and she twisted in her seat as much as possible. She spotted the white tip of Spike's tail wagging inside his kennel.

Bennett drove to a expansive, populated parking lot, and a sign overhead read Linkhalter Steel. He parked at the far side of the lot, farthest from the building, near a wide strip of grass. "Are you sure you're okay?"

Naomi's insides were wound tight as a crocheted knot. "Honestly, I'm a little shook up. Can you give me a few minutes to gather my wits?"

Bennett shut off the engine. "No problem. I'll check on Spike." He reached for the handle and shoved hard, but the driver's door refused to budge. After several shoulder thrusts, he surrendered. "It's stuck."

Several awkward seconds ticked by. Naomi realized Bennett couldn't get out until she did so that he could slide across the front seat. Unsure if her legs would hold her, Naomi exited the truck and leaned against the side panel. Her heart pounded hard against her chest.

Bennett released Spike from his steel kennel. "Great job, buddy." Bennett cradled the beagle in his arms, then gently set him on the ground. He ran his hands over the animal's body. "Not a mark on you."

Spike barked and wagged his tail in appreciation. He strode to Naomi and nudged her leg. She leaned over. "I'm okay, too. Thank you for asking," she teased, stroking his fur.

Bennett offered his arm for support in a gentlemanly fashion. The concern in his eyes and Spike's sweet disposition reduced her racing pulse to a normal rhythm. She linked her arm in his, grateful to have him steady her shakiness.

They strolled the perimeter of the pickup, stopping to inspect the driver's side where the guardrail had dented it with a massive crease.

"That explains why I couldn't open the door." Bennett's narration did nothing to enhance the sight. "Let's keep walking."

Sunshine warmed their skin as they sauntered the perimeter of the property. Naomi breathed deeply, filling her lungs with oxygen. Spike led the way to a grassy island, pausing to sniff the surroundings.

In less than the predicted time, two black SUVs pulled into the lot and parked on either side of Bennett's vehicle. Both marked units bore the same logo Bennett wore on his uniform shirt.

"There's Selena and Kyle," he announced.

Nervous, Naomi strode beside him as they approached the vehicles. A fit man wearing a gray shirt with the same MCK9 logo exited the first SUV. His thick, dark hair was cut short. Naomi didn't miss the way his brown eyes pierced her with unspoken questions, even from a distance. He moved to the rear door of his SUV and released a large dog with long, floppy ears. He snapped on a leash, and the animal strolled beside him, tongue lolling to the side as he paused, waiting for the woman also exiting her vehicle.

"What kind of dog is that?" Naomi whispered to Bennett. "Sort of resembles a bloodhound."

"Close," Bennett said. "That's Rocky. He's a coonhound trained in cadaver detection."

Naomi shivered at the thought of the animal finding a body.

Had Rocky found Peter? Sadness mingled with the unpleasant images in her mind.

From the other vehicle, an attractive woman with auburn hair emerged. She turned, fixing her green eyes on Naomi for a second before moving to the rear door. A brown blur bolted out of the SUV, then pranced around her. At her command, the dog sat, allowing her to secure a leash.

"That's Selena Smith and her Belgian Malinois, Scout," Bennett explained.

Naomi stiffened at the sight of the intimidating dog. "And his specialty?"

"Suspect apprehension."

"Great," Naomi muttered.

The team closed the distance between her and Bennett. Naomi realized they must've all considered her a drug-dealing serial killer, if they didn't still. "Um, do they think…?"

"That you're a murderer?" Bennett winked at her. "No, we've had meetings where I've updated everyone."

Naomi exhaled relief, yet she couldn't shake the sense they were sizing her up.

"Hi, Naomi. I'm Deputy Selena Smith." The woman extended her hand first. "This is my K-9, Scout." She gestured toward the Malinois.

Scout met Naomi's eyes in a silent warning. *Apprehension* meant if she tried running, she wouldn't get far. She swallowed hard. Duly noted. Naomi forced a shaky smile. "He's gorgeous."

"Don't tell him that." Selena grinned. "He's already got a big head."

The dog barked once and whined. The moment lightened the tension, and Naomi relaxed a little.

"See?" Selena rolled her eyes in a teasing reply.

"Rocky's biggest focus is food," the strange man replied.

At the mention of his name, the coonhound glanced up with soulful desperation.

"He looks hungry," Naomi commented.

"Nah, that's a total act. He just finished breakfast an hour ago." The man quirked a brow, feigning irritation, but a sparkle in his brown irises implied otherwise. "Hi, Naomi. I'm FBI Agent Kyle West." He didn't offer a hand to her. His daunting demeanor and title established their respective roles.

"It's a pleasure to meet you both, although I wish it were for other reasons," Naomi replied, suddenly cognizant of her arms hanging limply at her sides. Where was she supposed to put her hands?

The team engaged in discussion, using police terms, while Naomi focused on the animals.

The coonhound harrumphed, fluttering his long jowls, and glanced passively in her direction. Surely a cadaver dog was disinterested in the living. As opposed to his intimating friend, who looked like he could have her for lunch. The dog sighed and reverted his attention to Spike, offering a customary sniffing. He then sidled up to Naomi, as though confirming she was safe to be around while somehow defusing her nervousness. A grin tugged at her lips.

"Thanks for meeting us so quickly," Bennett said.

"Good thing we were close at the Windham Ranch when you called."

Naomi glanced up, catching Selena's gaze. She saw no challenge in Selena's eyes, but Naomi felt the weight of her curiosity.

"Let me catch you up." Bennett offered the team a synopsis of what had happened earlier, including the surprise of finding Naomi's van pulverized with bullet holes.

"Wow." Selena shook her head.

"Spike detected narcotics inside the vehicle near the same place where I found the two bags of fentanyl," Bennett continued. "Whoever did that to her van expected to retrieve their stash."

"Are there more?" Kyle asked.

"At this point, anything is possible," Bennett replied. "But the shooters drove a sedan. The truck that attacked us today was older, probably a seventies model, set high with a lift kit, push bumper and faded red paint. Doubtful you'll find them."

"Yep, your text offered that information," Kyle said.

Bennett shot Naomi a confused glance, and she shrugged. "I figured the additional description would help."

"Well done," Bennett replied. "You continue to surprise me."

Naomi's knees weakened at his approval.

"I reported the shooters to the local and state police. They've issued a BOLO for the vehicle." Kyle glanced down at his phone. "Speaking of. Just got a lead on the truck." He addressed his dog. "Rocky, let's go. We'll be in touch." The duo hurried back to their SUV and quickly departed the parking lot, leaving a dust cloud in their wake.

"We should probably go if we want to make your doctor's appointment." Bennett jerked his chin at Naomi, then addressed Selena, "I'll meet up with you and Kyle at my condo when we're done."

"Sounds good."

A contraction tightened around Naomi's middle, and she sucked in a breath.

Selena reached to support her. "What's wrong?"

Clearly, she'd not hidden anything from her expression. She waved off the deputy's concern with a forced smile. "Nothing more than Braxton-Hicks contractions." Naomi wrapped her hands protectively around her belly. "This little man is very busy." Not a lie, but she refused to draw attention to herself. The last thing Naomi wanted was returning to the hospital only to hear it was another false alarm.

Bennett moved closer, speaking to Selena, but standing nearer to Naomi. "They struck us on the driver and rear sides. She could have injuries."

"No. I mean. I'm fine," Naomi stammered as a case of uncontrollable shivers overtook her body. "I'm a little…shook up is all." Aware she was rambling but unable to control the erratic shaking, she said, "I'm sorry. It's just… I haven't…the hit."

"Shh, it's okay. Don't apologize. You're in the middle of an adrenaline dump, no doubt. Totally understandable. Just breathe deep." Selena spoke in a gentle tone, placing a hand at the small of Naomi's back. "Let's get you examined."

Though Naomi wanted to object, she feared her legs wouldn't hold her much longer. The last thing she needed was to fall.

"Spike can hang with Scout and me," Selena offered. She glanced at his pickup, pockmarked with bullet holes and dents. "Not sure that's safe to drive. I'll call for a tow truck and take you to the appointment."

"I can rent a car while we're at the doctor's office," Bennett said.

"I'll report it for you," Selena said. "You focus on Naomi."

"Thanks." They started toward Selena's SUV, and Naomi gave her a grateful nod. "Bennett?"

He turned to face her. "Yeah?"

"Maybe use a different impound lot," she teased.

"Roger that." He chuckled.

"And…" That was the last thing Naomi remembered before everything went black.

Bennett flipped through the same magazine he'd held since arriving at the obstetrician's office. The paper was a curled mess from his nervous twisting. He tried focusing on the case and contemplating potential leads. But his thoughts revolved around his concern for Naomi. She'd been in the examination room for an hour. Was that normal? She'd passed out after the car attack and quickly regained consciousness, for which he was eternally grateful. However, without discovering the reason she'd passed out, he couldn't relax. A brain injury? Internal injuries? His overactive imagination was stressing him out.

He'd utilized the time by pacing the waiting room, demanding updates from the cranky receptionist—who simply ignored him other than to say Naomi was fine and to please take a seat—and praying like he'd never prayed before that she and the baby were okay. At last, the door to the examination rooms opened, and he jumped to his feet as Naomi emerged. He tossed the magazine he'd pretended to read for the past hour.

"Are you all right?" His voice echoed, gaining him the attention of two women sitting nearby.

"I'm fine," she reassured in a whisper.

Her quiet rebuke reminded him he'd spoken louder than he'd intended.

Naomi checked out with the receptionist, and they exited the office.

Before Bennett burst, he blurted, "What did the doctor say? Is everything okay?" He led the way to the rental car—a white sedan—using the key fob to unlock the doors. "Did he explain why you fainted? Do you need to go to the hospital?"

"I told you it's good. I'm sorry I scared you." Naomi placed a hand over his forearm. If he wasn't so stressed about her condition, he might've focused on the way her touch sent his heart into an arrhythmia.

"What did the *doctor* say? Did he agree?" Bennett repeated, opening the passenger door and helping Naomi inside.

"*She*, Dr. Pankratz, did all the tests and monitored the baby's heartbeat. She confirmed I'm fine." Naomi withdrew her hand, and he missed it instantly. "Sometimes I pass out if my blood sugar gets too low, which is totally on me. I know better than to just eat cereal and not protein first thing in the morning." Naomi snapped on her seat belt, and he gently closed the door, then scurried to the driver's side and slid behind the wheel.

"Did the car attack hurt the baby?" Bennett asked, continuing the conversation. His stomach roiled.

"No, the baby's heart rate is normal. Little man ratted me out on my lack of nutrition. No more giving in to junk food cravings…at least not without adding something healthy."

Bennett exhaled relief. "Thank you, Lord." Being worried

about Naomi and the baby reminded him how out of touch he'd been with God lately. He'd just met her, and she had too big an impact on him—he'd explore that another time.

Regardless, he had to guard Naomi. Though his teammates could handle her protective detail, they'd more than proven themselves trustworthy, the idea of transferring her care to someone else was unbearable. Not with killer thugs relentlessly pursuing her.

Bennett merged away from the doctor's office and onto C-470 east and Interstate 25 northbound.

"Me too. I've had more excitement in the past two days than my entire life."

"The receptionist was close to tossing me out. I kept asking her if everything was okay. Like every five minutes. Toward the end, I expected her to call security."

"I'm touched by your attentiveness." Naomi chuckled, then the smile fell away. "I've been on this pregnancy journey alone from the start. It was nice to have the company today."

Bennett considered Naomi's strength and position. Even after facing the harsh realities of her husband's nefarious deeds, she maintained her kind disposition. In contrast, he'd grown bitter after Delaney Huxley, whom he'd shamelessly touted as the perfect woman to his coworkers and subsequently his fiancée, turned out to be the major drug dealer he hunted. That had changed him.

"I'm glad the receptionist didn't call the cops or have you thrown out. Though explaining why my arresting detective—who no longer held me as suspect—was having a conniption fit in the waiting room might've been awkward."

At the implication, Bennett grinned. "True." He loved Naomi's personality, her quick wit and teasing manner. *Stop that! She's off-limits!* He ran one hand over his head, squelching the thoughts.

"I'm unsure how this will play out with the men who are determined to kill me, but the doctor said I need to rest until the baby is born." Her hands caressed her belly. "I had a full schedule of tours. I can't afford to take the time off this close to the delivery date, but she said another incident or high stressor could bring on early labor."

"Didn't you leave open dates on your calendar in case you delivered sooner?"

"Unfortunately, that wasn't an option with no sick leave." She shook her head. "I scheduled up to my due date. My mom always talked about Evan and I being late arrivals. I don't expect to deliver early." Naomi shrugged. "I guess the truth is I didn't want to be sitting home alone twiddling my thumbs until little man arrives."

"I don't do well with idle time, either." Bennett's opinion of Naomi only grew better, but the poor woman needed to rest. "I'll help cancel your remaining tours."

"I'd appreciate that. Addy offered to handle my tours while I'm recovering from delivery. We'd talked about that as a backup plan in case little man came early."

"Smart! We'll tackle that first thing. Considering all that's happened, I'd prefer if you stayed at my condo. Selena and Kyle will assist in your protection detail."

"Thank you." Naomi seemed to relax slightly at his offer.

"I hate to drag us back to unpleasant topics, but can you think of any place the thugs might look for the drugs?"

"I have no clue." She grunted. "I was oblivious to my husband's activities." Naomi twisted in the seat slightly to face him. "Isn't it funny how you think you know someone so well, then discover you didn't know them at all?"

Bennett blinked several times. Thoughts of Delaney infiltrated his discussion like an unwelcomed visitor. The perfect timing also reiterated why he shouldn't have feelings for Naomi.

The realization hit him. He had feelings for her.

When had he lowered his heart shield? The emerging emotions weren't appropriate. Not only because she was his charge, but because of all that he'd endured with Delaney. "Yeah. It does. Are you angry?" He had no intention of blurting the question, but since the discussion was open, he pressed on, "Doesn't it make you want to distrust people and refuse to take them at face value?"

"Are you talking about Ted?"

Bennett shrugged. "In general."

"I'm angry that he put our lives at risk with his poor choices. It's hard to be on the receiving end of someone else's mistakes." She shook her head. "To answer your question, I can't live like that. Suspecting everyone all the time. That's exhausting. As my mother would've said, it puts you in prison."

"I'm not following you."

"If you hold on to bitterness and unforgiveness, withdraw from everyone and stay skeptical of people, you're putting yourself in a personal prison. The person who hurt you isn't suffering at all. Yet you live alone in the name of self-preservation. Ted owns his mistakes. They don't belong to me or those who enter my life after him."

Bennett swallowed hard. Naomi's words were like a splash of ice-cold water drenching his face. What she said made sense, but he bristled. He'd suffered at Delaney's choices. And until that moment, he'd never considered himself unrealistic. Since her betrayal, he didn't extend trust until the person had proven themselves first. That wasn't prison; it was wisdom. "I see it differently. Once you learn how untrustworthy folks are, you shouldn't be naive. You're required to make calculated decisions."

"Hmm, that's justifiable, too." Naomi shifted in the seat. "I'm sure in your profession, you can't take people at their word."

"Precisely."

"I'm a hopeless optimist, and Ted's bad choices won't change that. My baby deserves the opportunity to have a positive life outlook. I don't want to turn into one of those grumpy types who looks like she drinks lemon juice all the time. My mother said staying positive keeps the wrinkles away."

He chuckled. "Sounds like something my mom would say, too."

The highway was busy, and flashing lights ahead warned of an accident. They came to a stop, and Bennett glanced at Naomi. Her creamy skin and brilliant hazel eyes with gold flecks behind the green were enrapturing. He could get lost in them. Thankfully, she didn't seem to notice him staring as she leaned forward, peering out the windshield. "Wow, looks like a multi-car accident up there."

Bennett returned his focus to the road. "Yeah, it'll get uglier in rush hour."

She sat back in her seat. "Thank you for all you've done to help me and for willingly reviewing the evidence and proving the drugs weren't mine. I'm truly grateful. Without you watching over me, I'd probably be dead by now. But I would understand if you needed to transfer me to someone else's care. You've got better things to do than babysit me."

He sat speechless. He'd assumed the worst of her while she held him in high regard. Now she was offering him an out, and he wouldn't dare take it. His feelings for Naomi entered dangerous emotional territory.

Naomi's cell phone rang, and she reached to answer it. "Hey, Addy." A pause. She frowned. "Uh, yeah. I guess so. It's just temporary. But I'll be back at work soon. Right. Thanks." She disconnected. "Addy's a little pushy about sharing the proceeds of the tours she's handling for me. She's asking for a bigger share with an 85/15 split."

"Do you think she's involved with any of this? She stands to profit if you're no longer in business."

"I doubt it. You've checked into her, right?"

"Yes."

"See?" She yawned and covered her mouth. "Sorry, I'm tired."

"Rest. It might be a long drive with the accident up there."

"You don't have to tell me twice." Naomi leaned back and closed her eyes.

Bennett flicked a glance her direction, then focused on the road as traffic loosened and bottlenecked around the multi-car collision. Naomi's words pelted him with conviction, yet he clung to his strategy. Optimism was dangerous.

NINE

Naomi was contagious—at least her upbeat personality and kindness were. Bennett had distanced himself, opting to work on his laptop from his couch. The location provided a clear visual of the women seated at his dining room table. Their easy conversation and occasional laughter filled his lifeless condo with an unfamiliar lightness.

Based on Selena's demeanor and obvious ease around Naomi, Bennett wasn't the only one who enjoyed spending time with her. From where he sat, it was evident Naomi had won over Selena. She had a talent for endearing herself. Selena's guarded side had given way to a cautious but friendly attitude in the short time she'd hung out with him and Naomi.

The cursor on his internet search engine blinked, mocking his inability to focus. For the past hour, he'd pretended to busy himself, looking for updates pertinent to the RMK case and Ted Cavanaugh's death. He'd distance himself from Naomi in hopes of reigning in his bizarre and unwelcomed feelings.

So far, nothing had worked. His thoughts were on an endless reel, revolving around the beautiful mother-to-be sitting a few feet from him.

Bennett gazed over the top of his screen, studying Naomi. She fit in so well with his team, Spike and him. Even Scout had taken a liking to her. And all of it couldn't be more wonderful and horribly wrong. He didn't want, nor was he actively seeking, a relationship with anyone. Not that she'd demonstrated any interest in him. At nine months pregnant, her biggest focus was her baby. As it should be. What right did he have to entertain any romantic thoughts at this point in his life or hers? She deserved the best. That wasn't Bennett Ford. He was a broken, jaded, bitter workaholic. Crimes evolved and persisted without lessening, which allowed him to transition from one investigation to another. Never slowing down. He had plenty to deal with in the present regarding the identification and apprehension of the RMK. If they failed to find the killer, someone else—like Trevor Gage or any of his other friends—remained in danger.

If only Naomi's words hadn't created a fog of emotions around his mind and heart. She oozed encouragement, kindness and optimism. Her strong faith inspired him while making him question his cop sense. No one since Delaney had affected him the way Naomi did. And until he'd met her, Bennett was satisfied being alone.

Bennett caught Selena's disapproving frown in his peripheral vision and averted his eyes. Spike came to his rescue, bouncing at his feet. His whole back end wagged, thumping K-9 Scout's face with his tail. The Malinois lounged next to Bennett and gave Spike an annoyed harrumph.

"Sorry about that, Scout." Bennett hoisted Spike onto the sofa, lavishing affection on the beagle.

"Someone missed you," Selena said.

"It's not like I was gone for days." Bennett grinned. "He's not used to being away from me."

"Scout's the same way." Selena pushed away from the table and joined him in the living room.

Naomi did the same and slid into the recliner. "It must be wonderful to come home and have someone excited to see you."

Bennett caught the hint of sorrow in her tone, and he fought the urge to comfort her.

She leaned back and blew out a long breath. "Little man is growing like a weed and taking up all the space where my lungs are trying to work."

"I take it you know the baby is a boy?" Selena sipped a soda.

"Yes, but I'm keeping his name a secret until he gives his grand appearance. For now, I call him 'little man.'"

"That's cute," Selena replied. "Hopefully, you can rest until you deliver with no more gallivanting into wild car chases."

"No arguments here." Naomi chuckled. "You talked me into it."

"With all we've learned so far," Bennett said, taking the opportunity to launch into the investigation, "let's review the facts. It might spark a burst of brilliance and new leads."

"Agreed." Selena retrieved her laptop from her backpack and settled it onto her legs.

"How about brainstorming?" Bennett's gaze flitted between the women, and he noticed Naomi's slight wince. She averted her eyes. Not wanting to ask her the question he'd repeated ad nauseam, he opted for a fresh approach. "Before we get started, Naomi, do you need anything?"

At the mention of her name, Naomi looked up, lip quivering. Tears shimmered, and a blush covered her face.

"What's wrong?" Bennett tossed the laptop to the side and rushed to her. "Are you hurting? In pain?"

Naomi waved him off. "Ugh, stupid hormones. I'm fine. Just tired. Honestly." Her attempt to laugh emitted a forced grunt.

Selena passed her a tissue.

"Thank you. I never know when I'll start crying. It's super annoying." She dabbed at her eyes. "I'm grateful for the kindness you two have shown."

"I can't imagine all you've been through." Selena set a bottle of water on the coffee table nearest Naomi. She dropped onto the seat across from her, leaning forward.

Though he longed to comfort her, Bennett returned to the sofa.

"Others have endured worse. I'm not complaining," Naomi said. "God has seen me through the hard stuff. I'm never alone with Him. And as my mother would say, troubles keep me clinging to my faith, right?"

Troubles hadn't done that for him.

"Let's talk about the case. How can I help?"

"We should wait." Bennett glanced at Selena. She responded with an understanding jerk of her chin. "The doctor warned about stress," Bennett reminded Naomi.

"Pah. This isn't stressful. We're just talking." Naomi leaned back, adjusting herself on the recliner.

Spike hopped down from the couch and strolled to Naomi. "Well, hello there." She patted her leg. He sprung up, settling beside her.

"That's new," Bennett said. The dog's attention to Naomi and the warmness of the animal's compassionate gaze touched his heart. "As we discussed earlier, forensics confirmed Ted's fingerprints on the bags of fentanyl based on his concealed carry license permit."

"I can't believe I'd forgotten he had a gun." She blinked and shook her head. "I guess that shouldn't have surprised me. I try to think the best of everyone, especially those closest to me. His betrayal hurts."

Selena met Bennett's eyes as understanding of the Delaney debacle and her own experiences with her ex-boyfriend passed between them.

"On a positive note…" Bennett began.

"What? You're looking at the positive?" Naomi teased.

"Just this once. Don't get used to it," he quipped.

"Right." She grinned.

"Anyway, the forensic confirmations helped us to clear you from the possession charge," Bennett reminded Naomi.

"True. I appreciate that." She tilted her head in that endearing way Bennett had come to expect.

Selena inserted, "I'd like to talk about Ted."

"More?" Naomi blew out a breath. "What else can I share

with you that you aren't already aware of? In fact, you guys find things I'm oblivious to."

"You'd be surprised," Selena replied. "Our image or impression of Ted is based on what we learn through our documents and internet searches. Basically, boring one-dimensional Ted. You can offer us a view of his personality. The real Ted beyond his crimes."

"Yes," Bennett inserted. "What you share will help build his entire profile with nuances we weren't able to consider."

"That's logical." Naomi readjusted, but Spike didn't move. "Ted was outgoing, extroverted. We balanced each other well in that respect. He excelled at sales, so he did our promotional stuff. I preferred driving the van and connecting with the customers." Naomi resumed petting Spike, and he sighed contentedly.

Bennett wondered if his dog had dumped him. He grinned. Spike wasn't leaving Naomi's side anytime soon.

"What about before the business?" Selena asked.

"He was supportive of my rodeo-cowgirl performer career dreams. Riding was a big part of the reason I became a member of the YRC."

Bennett recalled Evan mentioning it in the interview he and Ashley had with him the month prior.

"No offense, Naomi," Selena said, "but after spending time with you, that's a big contrast to your personality."

Naomi chuckled. "Yeah, shy girls don't normally choose a spotlight career. Riding was different, though. Being on a beautiful horse gave me courage. I was in my own world."

"What changed those ambitions?" Selena asked.

"Ted and I began new dreams," Naomi said. "We wanted a business we could do together."

"That's understandable. A person's daily habits are telling, too," Bennett said. "Did Ted have any?"

Naomi took a few seconds before answering. "He loved to

jog in the morning—weather permitting. I was never a runner, so I didn't go with him. Not that he'd invited me to."

"Did that bother you?" Bennett asked.

"Nope. I appreciated our relationship independence." Naomi tucked a stray tendril behind her ear. "We had separate and collective interests. We wanted to be our own person instead of becoming one of those couples who cannot function without each other."

Bennett had once believed independent lives were healthy until Delany took advantage of him. Was it just another thing she'd exploited?

Selena regained his attention. "Were there any particular trails or areas he preferred?"

"His favorites were the foothills closest to our townhome."

Bennett made notes on his computer. "You mentioned that toward the end of his life, Ted had changed?"

"We'd talked about adding in nature trail hikes to our tour company, as I explained before," Naomi said. "A few weeks before his death, he spent a lot of time testing out trails. In retrospect, I have no idea if that was true."

"Addy just added nature hikes to her business," Bennett said. "That's sure coincidental. Was she aware you and Ted were also adding the feature before his death?"

Naomi didn't respond.

"You didn't go with him?" Selena asked.

"No, we had a full schedule. We used the divide-and-conquer method. Besides, I couldn't stop the tours to join him."

Naomi had trusted Ted implicitly. A common mistake Bennett recognized in marriage. Except, when did one take off their skeptical glasses?

Had Ted abused her trust by pretending to need time alone to hike? Or had the excuse provided him the perfect reason to get away by himself and conduct his nefarious drug dealings?

As though reading his unspoken question, Selena inserted,

"Don't most hikers use smartwatches and GPS apps on their phones?"

Naomi nodded. "Yes, Ted wore a smartwatch, and on the day he died—" Her voice hitched.

Neither pushed. They waited patiently as Naomi collected herself. "I provided the police with the recorded coordinates. They recovered his body nearby."

The details confirmed Bennett's assumption of her innocence. If Naomi had killed Ted, why deliver the location to the authorities? "Naomi, do you think Ted hid the rest of the stash or that he had something else they want—like records of deals or suppliers?"

She shrugged. "I suppose?"

"If he was hiding the drugs, the mountain trails provide endless places," Selena surmised.

"Are you saying he stashed them in the place where he died?" Naomi sat uprightly.

"I'd argue Ted did exactly that." Bennett activated a map on his computer, locating the site where law enforcement had recovered Ted's body.

"If he was in the process when the thugs showed up, he might've panicked," Selena said. "Or they tried to kill him, and he was running away—"

"As much as a person can while standing on the side of a mountain," Bennett interrupted.

"Then, in his haste to escape, lost his footing," Selena concluded.

Curiosity and questions lingered in Naomi's expression.

Excitement built within Bennett, and he jumped to his feet. "Selena, would you and Scout stay here with Naomi while Spike and I do some narcotic detection work?"

"Absolutely."

Naomi settled onto the sofa. "I wish Bennett would call, although I'm not sure how that'll affect the next course of events."

"Every lead draws us closer to catching the bad guys," Selena said. "Which in your case, means you can stop dodging drug-dealing enforcers."

"Right." Naomi reached for the bottle of water and took a sip. "I'm ready to disembark from the emotional and physical danger roller coaster."

"No one volunteers for that unwelcomed adrenaline rush."

Naomi tucked a throw pillow behind her back. "I'm beyond grateful Bennett didn't toss me in jail."

"Normally, he would've. He had sufficient evidence, too. Totally unlike him." Selena met her gaze. "Not gonna lie. I'd have arrested you and sorted out the details later."

Once more, she offered a silent petition of thanks. "Why didn't he treat me that way?"

"Bennett's not a spontaneous person. He weighed the situation, then acted applicably."

"He's an enigma," Naomi said.

Selena laughed. "That's one way to put it."

"Have you and Bennett known each other a long time?" The question escaped Naomi's lips before she'd processed how strange it might sound to Selena. At the deputy's quirked brow, Naomi quickly added, "I don't mean to pry."

Selena studied her for several uncomfortable seconds.

Had she overstepped some invisible discussion boundary? "Forget I asked. It's none of my business."

Selena closed the laptop and set it on the coffee table. "Bennett and I worked for different agencies, so the task force brought us together. We've sort of bonded over the shared experience of having our love interests betray our trust." Selena sipped from a bottled water. "I fell in love with a man who was later convicted of murder and sent to prison."

Another long pause overrode Naomi's quiet curiosity. "Was he guilty?"

"I don't know for sure." She crisscrossed her legs on the recliner. "I trust the judicial system. It's my life and how I make my living. To say I don't depend on it makes me a hypocrite."

"Yeah, but like most systems, there are flaws," Naomi reasoned.

"True." Selena sighed. "Part of me hopes—no—believes he's innocent. If he is, then I wasn't a fool to trust him."

"Self-preservation is understandable."

Selena grunted. "I'm a deputy. Trained to detect deception. Not seeing that in the person closest to me makes me either foolish or bad at my job."

"I disagree. Everyone has secrets." Naomi considered her statement. What had she withheld from Ted? The answer was easy. She'd never told him about the murders in Elk Valley. "Ted was the adventurous one. I happen to be in the jet wash of his choices."

"Been there, done that," Selena said.

"That sounds like experience talking."

Selena looked down, studying the water bottle. "I fell hard for Finn—that's his name—at the ripe old age of twenty-two. Of course, I thought I knew everything about him… Boy, was I wrong."

"Was there some part of you that questioned him?" Naomi shifted on the sofa. "I wonder if I missed signs?"

"I asked that same question."

Compassion for the deputy welled within Naomi. Scout strolled to the kitchen and sounds of him lapping water carried to them.

"Ugh, he's probably making a puddle." Selena set down her laptop and pushed out of the recliner.

Naomi watched as she entered the kitchen and groaned.

"Nice, Scout. Try to get some of the water in your mouth next time." Her teasing admonishment brought a grin to Naomi's lips. Selena gathered paper towels and bent to mop up the mess. "It's like having a furry child." Selena chuckled, resuming her position on the recliner.

"I understand. The beauty of loving someone is getting to be ourselves and not questioning everything?"

"That's the dream," Selena agreed. "If you could do it over again, would you still marry Ted?"

"Yes." Naomi answered without hesitation.

"Really?" Disbelief clouded Selena's face.

"Each experience is training for the next level of our journey." She rubbed her belly. Little man offered a thump of agreement. "Without Ted, this little guy wouldn't exist. And I wouldn't trade being his mama for anything in the world."

Naomi rose and walked to the sliding glass door, stepping onto the small deck. Bennett's condo sat on the outskirts of downtown Denver near the state capitol building. From her vantage point, she spotted a woman standing near the stoplight across the street. She glanced up as though sensing Naomi was watching her. The stranger didn't move, her position was almost a challenge.

From the height of the deck, Naomi had no chance of making out any details about the woman. Yet gooseflesh rose on Naomi's arms that had nothing to do with the spring breeze that fluttered her hair.

Something about her demeanor and stance seemed familiar. Naomi stepped closer to the railing, hoping to gain a better look.

A large delivery truck pulled up, waiting for the light to change. The woman disappeared into the building's shadow.

"Stop being silly," Naomi said aloud, then turned and re-entered the condo. Selena had her computer open again, so Naomi strolled through Bennett's open-concept home, saddened by the sterile decor. All of it screamed *temporary*. Aside from the essential furniture and accents like lamps and blinds, there were no paintings on the walls. No family pictures. No memorabilia or personal belongings. Bennett lived as though he could pack up and leave any day. Why? Did he fear putting down roots? Did his job not allow it? Naomi realized how little she knew about him.

"Is Bennett not planning on staying here?" Naomi moved to the sofa.

"Our positions with the Mountain Country K-9 Task Force mean we go where we're needed, though Denver is his hometown." Selena shrugged. "We're headquartered in Elk Valley, and our members are scattered across several states."

"I don't remember hearing about a task force when I lived there."

"We were brought together recently for the purpose of tracking down the Rocky Mountain Killer."

An involuntary shiver ran through Naomi's body. Her thoughts circled the overthinking drain. The future she'd once expected and planned for was gone. She looked around, realizing she also lived in the land of temporary. Would she ever go home again?

TEN

By the time Bennett and Spike arrived at Beaver Brook Trailhead outside the city of Golden, Colorado, Bennett was crawling out of his skin with eagerness. Though it was a weekday, visitors packed the place, forcing him to park a quarter mile from the trailhead. He'd expected nothing less. People flooded into Colorado from other states, overpopulating the beautiful grounds, in his humble opinion. Additionally, the number of passersby didn't bode with their initial thoughts of Ted concealing drugs here. Why not venture to a more private setting where multiple hikers weren't milling around?

Bennett used his phone to study the online trail map. Unless Ted had ventured deeper into the woods?

He turned slightly in his seat, utilizing his laptop set in the vehicle's docking station. Bennett surveyed Ted Cavanaugh's digital case file. A pair of hikers corroborated Naomi's account of Ted's GPS last known location when they advised seeing what appeared to be a human at the bottom of a deep ravine. Law enforcement had scoured the area and discovered Ted's body in the early morning hours of October 3. The medical examiner deemed Ted's fatality as accidental—a fall from the cliff. The autopsy listed Ted's cause of death as a severed spinal cord and noted several other injuries, including broken vertebrae, multiple lacerations, contusions and numerous fractured bones—the largest of which ascribed to his right arm and left leg.

Bennett's mind whirled. Had someone shoved Ted off the cliff after beating and possibly torturing him? The ME had requested no further investigation. He'd had no cause to.

Not until now.

He needed to survey the crime scene.

Bennett closed the laptop and exited his patrol unit. He released Spike from his kennel in the back seat, then snapped on the dog's harness and leash. He spotted a man standing close by, watching them. Based on the curiosity in his demeanor, Bennett anticipated his approach.

Sure enough, he stepped forward. "Cute dog," he said.

"Thanks," Bennett replied, tugging on his backpack and locking his SUV.

"You a cop?"

"Something like that," Bennett remarked.

"Cool. Is he like a search dog?" the man asked.

Bennett was used to inquisitive strangers. Spike got people's attention. "Yep, he's amazing. I just hold the leash."

"Whatcha searching for?"

"Today is a little different," Bennett said, diverting the discussion. "Out for a little R&R." Reconnaissance and Recovery, he thought, forcing away a grin.

"Cool." The guy lingered for a second. "Enjoy. It's a great day to be out," he said, walking away.

Bennett and Spike trekked the curvy road to the trailhead entrance. A posted sign designated Beaver Brook's trail level as moderate to advanced.

Bennett glanced down at his MCK9 uniform short-sleeved shirt and pants. He'd changed into hiking boots, but even Spike's MCK9 harness caught the attention of hikers as they passed. Bennett made light conversation but didn't linger. Other than a few nosy questions—which he tactfully avoided answering—he continued without stopping. When he neared the location where Ted's body was found, Bennett stepped from the trail into the forested area. He sought a better place to survey from, journeying deeper into the thick grove of trees bordered by craggy walls steeped high to one side.

From his position, the foliage provided concealment from hikers on the path. Bennett shifted his gaze to a flattened space where a gigantic boulder perched on the edge of the steep cliff. After double-checking his GPS coordinates on his cell phone to confirm he was in the correct place, he withdrew binoculars from his backpack. Bennett spotted an outcrop where the landscape leveled off slightly.

With Spike's leash snapped to his belt, Bennett hiked closer to inspect the area. The land transitioned, plummeting down a tapered ravine where sharp rocks and tree shrubs peaked up from the uneven gravel and dirt walls. Narrow, but not unpassable for a skilled hiker like Ted. The leverage also allowed him to remain hidden from witnesses. A surreptitious location to hide his stash.

Bennett surveyed the landscape, ensuring no one approached before he knelt beside Spike. He adjusted the K-9's harness, double-checking the leads were secured. "All right, Spike. Ready to search for some cookies?"

The beagle's thin tail swished with excitement.

"Let's find the cookies!"

With Spike in the lead, they carefully traversed the treacherous landscape. Bennett angled his feet to strengthen his stride as they descended the precipice. When they reached a space dotted with spiny plants and boulders in varying sizes, Spike tugged harder, aiming for a colossal stone. Bennett cautiously edged closer around the rough ground, vigilant to give Spike the leash length he needed.

To his surprise, Spike continued forward, descending the ravine and into a wooded area.

When they were fully concealed behind the foliage, Spike moved to a sizable rock. He barked twice in the distinct beagle sound, paused, and then barked once more. Just as Bennett had suspected.

Ted had buried the narcotics.

Bennett rushed closer and knelt. He glanced up, confirming their location was hidden from the hikers above. It took Bennett several tries before he rolled away the stone, exposing a soft dirt section. Withdrawing a small trowel from his backpack, Bennett dug into the rocky earth. After several minutes, the tip of the tool halted, tinging against something hard. Bennett dropped it. Using his hands, he brushed away the loose soil, revealing a metal box.

"Good job, Spike!" Bennett yanked the stuffed taco dog toy from his pocket and tossed it to the beagle.

While Spike enjoyed his reward, Bennett unearthed the container.

Voices drew closer. The beagle's ears perked up. Bennett lifted the binoculars. A pair of hikers passed on the path above, oblivious to him and Spike. Once they were out of sight, Bennett looped the binocular cord over his neck, letting them hang there. He donned latex gloves and opened the box.

Tiny amounts of familiar white crystals—fentanyl—littered the bottom, along with a folded piece of paper and a thick wad of cash. He lifted it, flipping through and counting. Mostly hundreds. The drugs were gone. Stolen? Moved? If so, why leave behind the money? Bennett carefully unfolded the paper. Messy script, indicative of a man's handwriting, centered the document.

I'm sorry, N.
To you and the baby. I got in over my head and they know
I want out. If anything happens to me, the dealer after
me is Roderick Jones and his henchmen.

I love you,
T

Beneath the letter, Ted had scrawled *Ecclesiastes 12:14*. Bennett grew up going to church but hadn't memorized his Bible that well. He'd have to follow up later.

Thunder rolled in the distance, and Bennett surveyed the darkening sky as rain clouds slowly stirred overhead. A soft breeze passed over him and a chill slithered down his back. Roderick Jones was a local criminal, a most-wanted celebrity. All the Denver metro area and surrounding law enforcement agencies kept Jones on their radar. Taking him down was akin to lassoing the golden goose.

Like one of those Plinko games, the pieces started falling into place. Ted had tried hiding the drugs, though his motive remained unclear. Either he'd intended to go to the police with the information, or he foolishly believed he'd outsmart Jones. He'd underestimated his enemy, and he'd paid with his life.

If Bennett didn't stop Jones, Ted's mistakes would cost Naomi and the baby's lives, too.

He used his cell phone to capture a picture of the note.

A rustling got his attention, and he looked up. Another roll of thunder warned of the impending storm.

Bennett returned the contents to the box and closed the lid, then placed it inside a plastic evidence bag along with his gloves, ensuring the fentanyl didn't contaminate his supplies. He sealed the bag before securing it inside his backpack, then added his trowel. Not wanting to waste a single second with the possibility of getting caught in the storm, he determined to call Selena on the way to DPD. He'd have to stop there first to drop off and log the evidence.

"Sorry, Spike, but you have to give me your taco."

With a few more quick squeaks, Spike relinquished the soggy toy into Bennett's hand. He tucked it into his pants pocket.

They hiked up from the ledge and started through the deep, forested trees to the hiking path. Bennett's new goal expanded. Not only would he take down the RMK, but he would finally get Roderick Jones and his cronies.

First, he'd have to break Naomi's heart with news of her deceased husband's deeds.

That elevated his blood pressure more than a hundred gunfights.

They'd reached a thicketed area when Spike stopped and barked, tail and hackles raised.

What had sent the beagle into a frenzy?

Bennett turned just as a slam to the back of his head thrust him into darkness.

Four hours had passed since Bennett's departure. Naomi's gaze flitted to the clock on the mantel. "Should we be worried that Bennett hasn't called yet?"

"No. The commute to Golden with traffic is lengthy by itself," Selena replied. "If he's hiking the area, that'll take time."

"But it's nearly dark out."

"Naomi." Selena's one-word admonition had her slinking into the kitchen, desperate to busy herself.

Naomi grabbed a dishrag and wiped the counter, mulling over the situation. She had no right to feel the strange emotions she did for Bennett. They'd just met. He'd planned to arrest her for being a serial killer. Yet she couldn't deny her concern for his safety and well-being. She'd lost Ted in those mountains. She couldn't bear to lose someone else she cared for.

She continued her contemplations while wiping down every inch of the small room when Selena's cell phone rang.

"Is it Bennett?" Naomi hurried to sit beside her.

"Yes."

Naomi leaned closer, making no attempt to hide her efforts to eavesdrop.

"Hey, what did you find?" Selena listened for several seconds, brow furrowing. "What? Are you or Spike injured?"

Naomi strained to hear. "What happened?"

"I think you should call for an ambulance, Bennett. Sounds like he hit you hard." Selena shook her head. "Fine, but I disagree."

"What's wrong?" Naomi blurted, heart racing.

"Bennett has an update for us." Selena set the device on the table between them and pressed the speakerphone option. "Go ahead."

"Can you hear me?" Bennett asked.

"What's wrong?" Naomi blurted. "Are you hurt?"

"I'll explain when I get there," Bennett responded. "Spike and I are fine."

"Now," Selena mumbled.

Naomi leaned closer to the phone. "Please tell me what happened."

"We're getting ready to leave Beaver Brook Trail."

"You've been there all this time?" Naomi asked.

"Yeah, our trip had a minor detour when someone attacked me. Before you flip out, I'm fine. Just a hard knock upside my head."

"At least you didn't hurt anything important," Selena teased, though Naomi noticed the worry in her green irises.

"Anyway—" Bennett dragged out the word for emphasis "—the best I can tell, I was out for about five minutes. It was long enough for the perp to get away," he grunted. "Apparently, Spike's barking got the attention of a hiker. He rushed to help us. Thankfully, the assailant didn't hurt Spike."

"Go straight to the hospital," Naomi blurted.

"Seriously, I'm fine. I need to tell you what we found."

Several seconds passed without another word. Naomi inched closer to the phone. Were they still connected?

"Now's not the time for suspense, Ford," Selena remarked.

"I had a nosy passerby when I first arrived. I didn't think much of it at the time, though looking back, he hesitated a little too long and asked questions about Spike and I." Bennett exhaled into the receiver. "Spike found a metal box buried near where Ted died."

"What was inside?" Naomi blinked, unsure what the discovery had to do with her. "I'm confused."

"About a hundred thousand dollars cash—smaller bills—

and a handwritten letter addressed to you," Bennett replied. "I'm texting Selena a picture of it. It's faded and might be hard to read. Whoever attacked me took the box."

"I could see them stealing the money, but why the letter?" Selena asked.

"It wasn't a random mugging. Someone followed me here, anticipating that I'd look for it and would find it with Spike's help. They'll be disappointed, though."

"Why?" Naomi asked.

"There were remnants of fentanyl, same cut as what I found in your van, Naomi," Bennett explained. "That's how Spike triggered on it to begin with. I think Ted buried the box and removed the drugs. I believe the money was intended for you."

"I'm struggling to grasp all of this," Naomi said. "Where would Ted get that kind of money?" Though even as she spoke the words, she knew the answer.

"The find adds to our suspicions that Ted was dealing," Bennett explained.

"It's a lot to absorb," Selena replied.

"Not sure I can handle much more," Naomi said.

Selena frowned. "I'm sorry you had to find out this way."

"Naomi, normally I would show this to you privately," Bennett said. "Because the information is imperative for us to work the case, I felt it was best to read it aloud. Selena must hear it, too."

Naomi inhaled a fortifying breath, bracing herself for what it would say. "How bad is it?"

"Selena, can you open the picture for Naomi?"

She raised the phone and swiped at the screen, gently placing it in Naomi's palm. A compassion she hadn't seen before in the deputy's face nearly undid her.

With a deep breath for courage, Naomi adjusted the device. Immediately, she recognized Ted's familiar scrawl. Like a voice from the grave, his words stretched out to her. Naomi's eyes welled with tears, blurring her vision.

"Naomi, does the handwriting look like Ted's?" Bennett asked.

"Yes." Her voice cracked.

Selena reached over and offered a light touch to Naomi's shoulder as she read the letter aloud. When she finished, silence hung in the air.

Naomi pressed her fingers against her trembling lips, trying to remember the scripture Ted had referenced at the bottom of his letter, and came up blank.

Selena swiped at her phone. "For God shall bring every work into judgment, with every secret thing, whether it be good, or whether it be evil."

"Hmm," Bennett said. "Confession?"

"Maybe. Roderick Jones!" Selena's enthusiasm confused Naomi.

"Who is that?"

"A big-time drug dealer," Bennett advised. "Someone I've chased most of my career. He's got long arms with a wide reach and escapes conviction."

"He's also extremely dangerous. No wonder you've been running for your lives," Selena added, cringing at the harsh reply. "Sorry, I didn't mean to put it that bluntly."

"But why come after me?"

"That's harder to explain. Ted must've moved the drugs that were in the box. I can't yet rationalize why. Unless it's the fentanyl from inside your van," Bennett clarified.

Naomi placed Selena's phone on the coffee table.

"Surely, Jones is aware you confiscated the drugs," Selena commented.

"Right. Or there are more that Ted hid somewhere else," Bennett said. "Naomi, can you think of any place we should consider?"

"He stayed at our storefront a few times, but that's nothing more than a tiny cube of an office."

Selena paced beside her. "Where did he live after moving out?"

Humiliation swarmed over Naomi. "I don't know. I tried to give him room, hoping that would help him find whatever space he searched for. I was so naive."

"No, you trusted your husband and took him at his word," Selena said.

"Keep brainstorming," Bennett said. "Jones wouldn't love losing his money, but it's not enough for him to come after you, Naomi. It's minnows in his ocean of crime."

"Ted intended to do something with the drugs he hid," Selena surmised. "Sell them?"

"Negative. His reasoning isn't clear, but maybe he planned to hand them over to the authorities. If Jones figured out he'd lost Ted's devotion, he'd take whatever means necessary to eliminate him," Bennett explained. "Ted's death wasn't an accident. He premeditatedly buried this box. It took time and planning to find the right place. Jones or his henchmen probably followed or traced Ted to the location. If he refused to give up the information, they may have tortured him, then thrown him off the cliff."

Naomi's stomach roiled at the images. "I'm not sure if I'm angry that he was involved in such a mess or confused why he didn't go straight to the authorities. Worse, why not come to me and tell me the truth? We could've worked through it together," Naomi said. "But why are Jones and his cronies still coming after me?"

"Jones's henchmen may have thought Ted told you where he'd hidden the drugs or that you knew of Ted's plan," Selena replied.

"So why wait six months after his death?"

"In line with Selena's rationale, they've probably watched you for a while. Which means they've watched me watching you, so they had to be careful and tread wisely," Bennett explained. "They figured—as we had—that if they gave you space and let you take the lead, you'd show them what they wanted. Your predictable schedule baffled them. You weren't buying expensive things or acting any differently than you had since before Ted's death. They waited to see what you'd do." Bennett's voice grew softer. "When you went to Peter's ranch, it was outside of your normal routine."

"They assumed I had the drugs with me, or that I'd hidden them on the property or in my van," Naomi concluded. "Is the stress getting to me, or is that logical?"

"You're reasoning like a cop." Selena patted her hand. "It makes sense."

"I still don't understand why or how Ted got involved in this." Naomi sighed.

"You mentioned his concerns about finances," Bennett began. "If he connected with Jones or any of his low-life cronies, they probably promised Ted he'd bring in more money than he'd ever make in the tour business."

Naomi bristled. Was he seriously justifying Ted's crimes?

"Drugs lure lots of unsuspecting people into a world beyond their control," Selena agreed. "They make tiny compromises, and before they know it, they're in deep."

"Selena is dead-on accurate. I've watched it happen many times in my career, Naomi. Money is that lying voice that promises things it can never deliver." Bennett's comment spoke of experience, along with a deeper knowledge she couldn't quite put her finger on.

With countless thoughts bouncing around in her head, she could scarcely think straight.

"Worse, once Ted was in Jones's inner circle, there was no way out," Bennett expounded. "Jones isn't someone you want to mess with. I'm sure Ted feared for his life and yours. He was coming to a dead end—sorry, no pun intended."

"Or he hid them in advance, then Jones and his henchmen demanded the return. They take him back to the site, but Ted is uncertain where he buried them. Or he lied," Selena offered.

"Maybe he tried running, they pursued, and he fell. That's still not an accident, though."

"Yes, that's plausible, too. Whatever the case, they're responsible for Ted's death. I intend to add that to their long list of accumulating charges," Bennett said. "It's pure speculation, since we don't have evidence of what happened that day. Ted hiding the fentanyl says to me he was trying to get out of the mess he'd gotten into."

"Wow." Naomi put her head in her hands, trying to contain the absurd amount of information. "This is a living nightmare of a true crime show. Whose life looks like this?"

"It's a lot to process," Bennett said. "Ted clearly wanted you to have the note and the money. Obviously, something stopped him from telling you where it was, but he must've regretted his actions."

Was that a comfort? "What happens now?"

"We work on the case," Selena replied. "You rest and deliver a healthy baby."

"While we keep you safe," Bennett answered. "I need to stop at Denver PD, so I'll update the rest of the team from there. It'll take me a while, but I'll be back ASAP."

"Roger that." Selena exhaled. "I'll type up the details in the case file."

"See you soon." Bennett disconnected.

Naomi jumped to her feet and paced the small living room, catching the attention of Scout and Spike. The dogs both sat in sphinx poses, watching her. "Excuse me."

She walked to the bathroom, desperate for a few moments alone to process the mess of her life. She closed the door and stood with her hands flat on the countertop and studied her reflection in the mirror.

Every single part of her marriage with Ted floated in an abyss of unexplained questions. Naomi wept as the sting of betrayal infiltrated her heart. While she'd planned a future for their baby, in a loving home where she'd dedicated herself to being a wife and mother, Ted had looked her in the eye and deceived her. Not just once, but over the course of months, years maybe—so many times that she wondered if he'd ever told the truth.

ELEVEN

After praying, peace had settled over Naomi. God would take care of her.

She returned to the living room, where Selena worked on her laptop. "Hanging in there?"

"Yes. I had a good cry. At least this time it's not just hormones." Naomi crossed her arms. "Once Jones gets the drugs Ted hid, he'll kill me."

"We won't let that happen."

"Someone attacked Bennett!" Naomi snapped. "If they got to him, how will you protect me?"

"The MCK9 task force is good. We'll get justice for Ted and for you. I can't promise when, but we won't stop until you're safe."

"I appreciate it, but I'm also enough of a realist to accept that Jones has eluded capture all this time for a reason."

To her credit, Selena didn't argue.

Images of someone shoving Ted off a cliff ratcheted her pulse.

Naomi walked to the dining room and sat down. Placing both elbows on the tabletop, she steepled her fingers. "Selena, I'm aware your team can't protect me indefinitely."

"Correct, as much as I hate to agree."

"I need practical advice on where to go from here. Do I move away, change my name? How do I protect myself and my baby?"

"Let's take one step at a time. If we're forced to consider other options, we'll deal with it then."

Naomi stared at the table's pattern.

How clueless was she to miss Ted's transgressions? The man she'd married wouldn't use or deal drugs. What changed?

Images of Ted's desperate state of mind brought on a wave of sorrow over Naomi. She couldn't help but pity him. If he'd let her into his troubled world, things could've been different.

Naomi bowed her head. "Lord, I don't know what to do with all of this. It's too much of a weight for me to bear by myself."

"Amen." Selena rested a hand on her shoulder. "You're not alone."

Naomi swallowed the emotion clogging her throat. Her stomach tightened. How was she supposed to avoid stress with the never-ending barrage of unbelievable facts thrown her way? She inhaled deeply, calming herself against her rising emotions. Little man kicked, fully engaged in his daily round of baby aerobics. All that mattered was ensuring she stayed healthy for the sake of her child. Ted was gone. Regardless of what he'd done, or his reasons, nothing had changed.

Naomi offered a prayer of thanks for Bennett and Selena. They'd worked hard to help her find the truth. She had to trust someone. For now, that meant trusting them.

Her thoughts returned to Bennett. The mysterious detective. She replayed Selena's comments about how differently he'd treated Naomi.

Selena walked back to the recliner.

Naomi walked to the kitchen, opened the cabinet, withdrew the box of cereal, and then poured some in a small bowl. She headed for the living room.

"Snack time?" Selena smiled.

"Nervous energy."

She took a bite, trying to distract herself from her racing thoughts. "I wonder if I'll be enough for this little man," Naomi admitted, rubbing her belly. "He will need a father, and I can't be that for him. My brother is wonderful, but he works a ton, and I'd never ask him to shoulder that responsibility."

Selena met her gaze.

"I assumed we were headed in the right direction. He was going in another. Turns out, Ted and I had no future. I was the last one to realize it."

Scout strolled into the room and dropped beside Selena. "I guess we never really know the people in our lives. We imagine we do, but they can sure surprise us. You're not the only woman to be blindsided by her significant other."

Naomi snorted. "Nobody is as oblivious to their spouse's activities as I was."

"Remember, I was in love with a convicted murderer." Selena tilted her head. "Bennett had a similar experience with his ex-fiancée."

Naomi nearly choked on the cereal at the word *fiancée*.

At her stunned silence, Selena's eyes went wide. "Or…did he not mention that?"

"No. He didn't." Naomi gaped, hoping she wouldn't clam up.

"Guess that wasn't my story to share," Selena mumbled. "I just assumed…with the three of us having such similar experiences…"

"I don't want you to violate any confidential information, but would you be willing to tell me some of his story?"

Selena paused. "I'll only tell what's in the court documents. Bennett found out Delaney was the drug dealer he was tracking."

Whoa. Naomi pondered Ted's betrayal. "I can't imagine how that hurt Bennett."

"Yeah, it made a huge impact. Bennett's more guarded and jaded than I am. And that's saying a lot." Selena exhaled. "He doesn't trust easily. However, the experience also gives him understanding of your position."

Naomi nodded mutely.

"Now that I've revealed stuff I had no business sharing, is it too much to ask that you forget everything I said?" Selena joked.

"I have a lot going on in my life at the moment, so it's possible." Naomi chuckled. "Bennett seems like a private person. I'm that way, too. Not that I have a lot of folks to share my life with." In the years she'd lived in Colorado and prior in Elk Valley, Naomi hadn't had many friends besides Peter. "I had a hard time making friends as a kid. It's worse as an adult. Especially when you find you don't want to tell anyone details about your life."

"I get that."

"I keep to myself, although in this case, that's beneficial. How would I explain that my husband died hiding drugs from a lethal dealer?" Naomi gave a bitter laugh.

"Might be a great icebreaker for new friendships," Selena teased.

Naomi giggled despite the seriousness of the topic. "Right? I probably shouldn't bring it up in mother-and-baby groups. I'm not sure they'd invite me again if I blurted that."

Selena guffawed. "I'm sorry. I don't mean to minimize your situation, but thank you for making me laugh."

"Laugh or cry. I figure those are our only options here."

"True." Selena blew out a long breath and took a sip of water. "Well, sadly Bennett and I both understand."

"You realize that's abnormal?"

"I'm submersed in law enforcement life. I forget the rest of the world isn't like us. On the other hand, as you see, you're not the only one." Selena gestured in a ta-da manner from her chair. "We've had exes who weren't who we thought they were."

"Maybe there's still hope for us optimistic romantics."

"I'm not sure I'd classify myself as optimistic or romantic. At least not anymore." A sadness appeared in Selena's green eyes.

Naomi surveyed Bennett's condo again. The lack of personal adornments and pictures made sense now. When Ted had moved out, then died, she'd kept only the single picture of them together. Everything else brought back painful memories.

"Bennett's a great guy, but he's committed to the job," Selena added.

Naomi heard the hint, but it didn't stop her from speaking the next words. "Most definitely. He's easy to be around, protective, comforting, engaging in conversation. His sweet disposition reminds me what it's like to be cared for in ways I'd forgotten were possible. It's as though we've known one another forever."

"Dangerous events can influence romantic thoughts. It's that need to survive that comes with facing trauma. Emotional transference."

Naomi averted her gaze. "And he's devoted to his career."

Why had she revealed her crush on Bennett? Her cheeks flushed. "I'm sure taking on an already established family—" she gestured toward her belly "—isn't on his agenda." Naomi realized her comment sounded like she was baiting Selena for information. "Not that any man would be interested," she blurted.

"Who knows?" Selena lifted her hands in mock surrender. "Just keep your expectations low."

Naomi nodded, disappointment clouding her heart. She caressed her belly, reminded again that God had given her a precious baby to care for.

He was her biggest priority.

Her only priority…besides staying alive.

Selena's cell rang. "Yep," she answered, rushing to the front door.

Naomi sat up straighter, unsure what was happening.

The familiar coonhound entered, panting softly beside his FBI agent partner, who carried a large pizza box. He also balanced a cardboard drink holder containing cups of ice cream on top.

Naomi struggled to remember both his and the dog's names.

Selena rescued her from embarrassment. "Kyle, I've never been more grateful to see you." She lifted the ice cream container.

"Rocky, go chill by Scout," Kyle said. "Hey, Naomi." He walked to the dining table and set down the pizza box.

"Hi." Unsure if she needed to use his title, first or last name, she stuck with the single-syllable greeting and rose to join them.

Girl talk with Selena had ended, but Naomi's disappointment faded with the aroma of food and the affirmation that Bennett Ford was off-limits.

Night had fallen when Bennett arrived at his condo. For the first time since returning to Denver in pursuit of the RMK, they'd made progress. Granted, it wasn't toward that case, but he'd take the lead on Roderick Jones as a win.

Bennett released Spike from the vehicle and snapped on his leash, giving him a short walk before they headed upstairs. Selena had texted Bennett, advising Naomi was already in bed so he wouldn't wake her.

Disappointed, Bennett strolled to his front door. The strange emotions swirled in his mind. Why did it matter that he wouldn't get to talk to Naomi tonight? She was nothing more than his charge.

Yet he had looked forward to seeing her.

"Get a grip, Ford," he mumbled, punching the elevator button.

Spike sat and turned, glancing at him.

"Don't say it. I already chastised myself."

The beagle snorted, and they entered the elevator. By the time the doors opened again, releasing him to his floor, exhaustion settled in. Maybe he'd finally get a good night's rest.

Bennett unlocked the door and walked into his condo.

"Hey." Selena looked up from where she sat on the sofa, working on her laptop. "That took longer than expected, huh?"

"Happens every time I go into the DPD lab. Eduardo—"

"The crime tech lab guy?" Selena asked.

"Yeah, he and I got to talking. How'd the evening go?"

"Good. Naomi and I chatted, and Kyle brought pizza and ice cream."

"Please tell me there are leftovers." Bennett's mouth watered. "I haven't eaten tonight."

"Yep. There's plenty in the fridge and freezer, respectively."

Bennett walked to the kitchen to wash his hands. "Where is Kyle?"

"He returned to the hotel to work out before crashing for the night." Selena closed her laptop and got to her feet. "I've spent most of the evening going through the lab results from Peter Windham's crime scene. Just like Henry Mulder's Montana barn, there's nothing substantial. No fingerprints. No strange plants or things that are out of the ordinary for the area. The RMK was careful not to leave any trace behind."

"If only that shocked me," Bennett replied sarcastically, pulling out the pizza box from the fridge and setting it on the counter. He opened the lid. "What's all the green stuff on it?" He wrinkled his nose.

Selena approached with a grin. "Uh, those are called vegetables, Detective."

"Ha ha. What kind is it?"

"Veggie with a light crust." Selena closed her laptop.

"What's the point?" Bennett lifted a slice, inspecting it. "That's not pizza. Where are the layers of cheese and pepperoni?"

Selena chuckled. "Welcome to grown-up pizza."

Bennett took a bite, and though he had to admit it tasted good, he wasn't giving in easily. "Catch me up on the evening."

He strode to the living room and dropped into the chair opposite Selena.

"Here's where I need to apologize. I may have stuck my foot in my mouth."

Bennett chewed while Selena provided a short rundown of the discussion she and Naomi had regarding Delaney. Bennett paused, picking at a stray olive. Though he'd prefer not to share the intimate details of his personal life, it was better Naomi knew the truth.

"I assured her you're not in the market for romance," Selena concluded.

"Why? Was she implying she was interested in me?"

A sparkle in Selena's eyes said she'd picked up on his not-so-subtle way of fishing for information.

"I mean, if she was, you heading that off was smart," he said between bites of pizza. Did he really believe that?

"Are you sure?"

"Yes. Yeah. Most definitely." He infused appreciation into his tone while silently questioning the strange sense of disappointment. Naomi was off-limits for too many reasons. "The last thing I need is another failed relationship."

"That's what I figured you'd say."

"Kinda preferred Naomi didn't hear my pathetic history for getting buffaloed by a heartless wonder of a criminal." He swallowed and took a sip of soda. "But it's fine."

Selena winced. "Again, I'm sorry for overstepping. Just remember, you're in good company. It seems the three of us have a common connection in that department." She patted his shoulder. "And I'd say we are all intelligent, competent people, so it's not a personal defect."

"You're just saying that to make me feel better," Bennett grumbled, but he appreciated it anyway.

"Nope. It's as true for me as for you." Selena sighed. "I'm going to head out for the night. We should touch base first thing in the morning with the team. I haven't heard from anyone since notifying them about your mountain adventure, so I'm guessing there are no updates on the RMK or Cowgirl."

He nodded. "Good night." Bennett walked her and Scout out, locking the door behind her. Spike trailed them, tail wagging. "Hungry, buddy? Yep, you want dinner, too."

He led the way to the kitchen, pulling out Spike's food.

After filling his bowls and washing his hands again, Bennett finished the last piece of pizza.

He glanced at the clock. It wasn't that late. Would Isla still be working? Bennett sent her a text, and she quickly responded, agreeing to a video chat. Bennett carried his laptop to his dining table and logged in, inserting his EarPods to prevent waking Naomi.

"Hey, sounds like you had a busy day," Isla said once they were connected.

"It's satisfying to have something to move forward with. Even though this isn't where we were headed."

"Yeah, unbelievable Roderick Jones is involved. What're the chances?"

"In this area, decent. He's been running drugs hard here for a while."

Isla leaned back in her seat. She looked calmer than when they'd last spoken.

Bennett took the opportunity. "When we spoke earlier, you seemed a little distracted. Everything all right?"

"Sorry about that," Isla said. "This whole foster parenting thing is complicated."

"How're things going with the placement?"

"I expect to hear any day about when they'll bring me the newborn. I cannot wait to be an official foster mother!" Isla beamed from the other side of the screen.

Bennett smiled at her enthusiasm. She'd make a great parent. Images of Naomi and Isla talking about their children's first milestones bounced to mind. He blinked and shook off the strange thoughts. Where had that come from?

"I promise I had a reason for pestering you at this time of night," Bennett began.

"Aw, now I'm hurt. It wasn't just a friendly chat?" Isla teased.

Bennett grinned. "Well, that too. I really did want to check in and see how you're doing. I also hoped you'd work your mad tech skills for me."

"Always."

"In talking with my pal Eduardo down at the DPD lab, I kept circling Ted Cavanaugh's involvement. Can you dig into his background?"

"Absolutely."

"Just holler at me if you find anything good."

"Are you looking for something specific?"

Bennett sighed. "Yes and no. In the short time I've gotten to know Naomi, I cannot reconcile how she'd be involved with a deadbeat druggie. That tells me either Ted was a phenomenal actor, or a significant event or situation changed him. Money is a huge motivator for crimes, but it's not enough for this case."

"I'll drill down to his kindergarten enrollment years," Isla quipped.

"You're the best."

A fun ring tone chimed, and Isla glanced down. "Oh, that's my phone. It's the agency!"

Without exiting the call, Bennett listened as Isla answered. Her broad smile faded, replaced by down-turned lips and creased eyebrows. "What?" she said, panic suddenly in her voice. "But that's not true! None of it!" She listened more and seemed to calm down a bit. "Oh, I see."

Bennett leaned closer, feeling guilty for eavesdropping but concerned about his teammate's obvious distress.

"I understand. Yes, of course. Thank you." Isla set the phone down and looked at him. "My application to foster the infant— or any child—is postponed indefinitely." She swallowed hard and her lip quivered.

"What? Why?" Bennett asked, then mentally berated himself for interrupting her.

"Apparently, the agency received an anonymous report from a caller who claims I have drug and alcohol addiction issues. The person alleged witnessing me do both, starting in the morning and going throughout the day!" Isla's voice rose, anger replacing the sadness. "They're giving me a chance to rebut the accusations, but it'll take time."

"That's—" Bennett ground his teeth to keep from saying anything his mother wouldn't approve of. "Come on! That's so wrong! You work in law enforcement."

"Yeah, but what can I do? It's my word against this horrible accuser."

"Offer a drug test. Tell them the team will vouch for you."

Isla nodded. She leaned forward, and he saw the pain in her eyes. "Bennett, I've never touched alcohol or done any drugs. What is going on? And why didn't this totally fabricated report come up in my background checks during the certification process? Why now?"

"Exactly." Bennett's cop brain sped into action. "Why would someone want to stop you from fostering or adopting?"

"If I could answer that, I would. Who hates me that much?"

"No enemies come to mind?" Bennett probed.

"No, but don't you say everyone has enemies?" Isla gave a bitter snort. "Even if they're unaware?"

He winced at the repetition of his cold but accurate belief. "Isla, think hard. Is there anyone who found out about your foster-to-adoption journey who wasn't on your list of references? Someone who would take that as an affront?"

Isla considered his question and shook her head. "No."

Who would be so cruel as to interfere with Isla's benevolent dream? "Anyone who's been around you for more than a day knows how important this is for you."

She lifted her chin. "Well, whoever this person is, they're not getting away with it. I'll investigate it myself."

"That's the right attitude. Holler at me if there's anything I can do. I'll be thinking about ways to help too," Bennett assured.

"Thanks." Isla yawned. "I will."

"Get some rest."

"You too. Good night."

They disconnected, and Bennett closed his laptop. For every victory their team gained, there was another defeat. Would it ever end?

TWELVE

Naomi joined Bennett on the morning walk with Spike. "That sunrise is captivating."

"Agreed." Bennett shot her a smile, and she fought her knees to keep from weakening.

They hadn't solved Ted's murder or discovered anything new since the day before, but she felt optimistic.

"Lost in thought?" Bennett asked.

"A little. Is Selena coming over today?"

"Yes, she and Kyle will be here around lunchtime to go through evidence and work the case."

"Oh, good. I enjoyed talking with her last night. Sorry again for crashing early. The day's events caught up with me."

"Don't apologize. You're supposed to rest," he reminded her gently. "I'm glad you got some sleep."

"I did. Like a rock. Guess I'd better soak up as much of that as I can before little man makes his appearance."

"I can't offer any personal experience, but from the stories I've heard, yeah, you're going to want to bank energy for later."

They waited as Spike paused to sniff a row of flowers. Naomi's gaze roved the area where many houses had neatly manicured lawns awakening to spring. A woman dressed in leggings and a short-sleeved shirt jogged on the opposite side of the street. Despite Naomi's wave, the woman, who wore mirrored sunglasses and had EarPods inserted, was too focused on exercising to return the gesture.

Naomi glanced down, determined to add in exercise in her own life as soon as possible.

If only she'd be sharing the joys of motherhood with Bennett. *Ugh.* Why wouldn't those thoughts leave her alone?

He turned to face her. "Will you have any help with the baby?"

The man had an uncanny way of tackling contemplations before she spoke them. Naomi shook her head. "No, but I'll be fine. Once I return to work, it'll be nice to have little man ride along with me. I'll enjoy his company when I'm driving the tour bus. I mean after I get a new one. Thankfully, the insurance should cover the cost of the replacement, right?"

"I hope so."

Spike continued forward, and they resumed the stroll.

"You're going to take the baby with you on your tours? Won't that be hard?"

She shrugged. "It'll be challenging until we get a routine down, and I won't be able to do it every day. I have a daycare lined up, but the thought of being away from him tears at my heart." Naomi didn't add she couldn't afford full-time daycare. That wasn't Bennett's concern, and she'd troubled him enough with her personal problems. "I'll have to get used to being a working parent."

"Did your mom work outside the home when you were growing up?"

"Yes, part time. Somehow, she was always there for us, though. I don't know how she did it." Naomi recalled talking to her mother after school. Most teenagers wouldn't have spent their time in parental chats, but Naomi had enjoyed it. "She was my best friend. I miss her every single day."

"My mom is great, but I don't see or talk to her as much as I should." Bennett groaned. "Now I feel guilty."

Naomi chuckled.

"Tell me about your family."

"We were close, probably because there were only four of

us. My parents were supportive if Evan and I wanted to try new things. Especially when I started rodeo performance stuff."

"Do you miss riding?"

"All the time. It was freeing." A soft breeze fluttered her hair, and she tucked strands behind her ear. "If only horse care and upkeep weren't so expensive."

"Did your brother also ride?"

"No, not really. We've always moved in our own circles."

"Totally get it."

"After my parents' deaths, I was lost."

"The accident happened five years ago?" Bennett asked.

"Yes. Ted was a lifeline for me. We weren't married yet, just dating, but he was supportive and kind."

"The picture you paint of Ted differs from the one in my mind."

"I'm sure. I don't know how he got involved in the mess he did, but I'm convinced he wasn't always like that."

"Naomi, I agree with you."

She stopped and faced him. "You do?"

"We're digging into Ted's life to explain the strange clues."

"Ted didn't have any living family and never talked about his past. He was touchy about it, and I only know his grandmother raised him."

"Where did he grow up and attend school?"

"He said he was from Denver and attended Northridge High School."

Bennett frowned. They started walking again. The older neighborhood's bungalows had established lawns. Birds trilled from the trees that towered overhead.

"Do you think he was lying?"

"I didn't say that. But I'm going to check it out. Did Ted have family in the area?"

"No," she replied, sadness sweeping over her. "His parents died when he was young. His grandmother—also deceased now—raised him."

Spike traversed the sidewalk, tail high and a bounce to his canine step.

"I'm sad little man won't have any living grandparents," she admitted.

"There's not much in the case file about your parents' deaths. But we don't have to talk about that if you don't want to."

"No, it's okay." Naomi sighed. "They were driving home on a winter night. They never should've been out at that time in the first place, but my dad always aided whoever was in need. When his buddy's water heater went out, my parents offered to help install a new one. The blizzard arrived earlier than predicted. The water heater installation didn't go easily—basically, the perfect storm. They hit black ice and dad lost control, rolling the car. They were both killed instantly." Her throat tightened.

"I'm so sorry." Bennett's tone held compassion, which only made the moment worse.

They walked on for several minutes before Naomi continued, "My mom oozed kindness. She took casseroles and pies to neighbors in need or just because. She would've been a wonderful grandmother. My dad was quiet, but strong and loving. I pictured him bouncing my son on his knee while regaling him with his exaggerated fishing adventure stories. I'm sad they're not here to celebrate this milestone with me."

"It's only you and Evan now?"

"Yeah."

"Will Uncle Evan be a big part of your child's life?" Bennett asked.

"He's got his job recruitment firm in Elk Valley—which you probably already know. He's super busy with that."

"Will you visit him?"

"Doubtful, until the baby is older." She crossed her arms over her chest, tugging her cardigan closed. "I have no desire to return to Elk Valley."

"Even for the reunion?" Bennett asked.

Naomi considered the question. "I'd toyed with the idea when I first got the invitation."

"What changed?"

"Honestly, going to Peter's ranch solidified my reasons. It's all reminders of that part of my life." Naomi bit her lip, contemplating. "Talking it out helps. I'm curious to see how everyone has changed. And to find out what they're doing now, but being in Elk Valley, especially after losing my folks, is…hard."

"I understand that."

Spike stopped again to investigate an unfamiliar smell.

"Well, hopefully your brother will visit you."

"Evan comes when he can, usually a couple of times a year."

"Why didn't he leave Elk Valley?"

"He's a creature of habit." Naomi chortled. "Evan is rooted and hates change."

They rounded the block and headed back toward the condo with Spike in the lead.

"Spike has me missing the joys of owning a pet," Naomi admitted. "Living alone, I might reconsider a canine protector. Not that I could handle caring for anyone else right now."

"Maybe when your son is older," Bennett replied.

Spike paused again, and they stopped, waiting for him to finish his exploration.

"After watching Evan's grief over losing his dog, Kiko, I'm unsure my heart could endure it." At Bennett's quirked brow, Naomi explained. "She was his female chocolate Lab. He did everything—to the extreme—to help her through her illness. Her death devastated him. The man is a dog lover to the max." Naomi whispered, "Don't tell him I told you that. He'd kill me for divulging his softer side."

Spike advanced, allowing them to continue walking.

Bennett chuckled. "Your secret is safe with me."

"I knew I could count on you." She winked and their hands brushed. Naomi scooted away. "Spike's made me realize I have a canine shaped hole in my heart."

Bennett grinned. "I have a feeling you're going to be very busy soon."

"Yes. It won't be the traditional family I had hoped for, but it'll be good." Naomi thought about the baby's arrival. Recalling the destruction of her possessions, especially the nursery, caused a wave of sadness to course through her. "When will law enforcement release my apartment?"

"I'll follow up with the department today." Bennett hesitated.

"What aren't you saying?"

"They should've released the scene, but it's not safe for you to go there right now."

Naomi caressed her belly. "I'm sort of on a fixed timeline here."

"I'm working on it, I promise."

They paused outside Bennett's condo building door as a couple exited, holding hands. Naomi exchanged a smile with the woman as they walked by.

Naomi's heart squeezed, reminded that she was alone. "Do you want a family of your own someday?" The question escaped her lips before she stopped it, and she longed to rewind the moment. The other part of her recalled all that Selena had told her. What if Selena was wrong? Had Bennett's heartbreak over Delaney destroyed his dreams?

They reached the elevator as the doors opened. A second couple entered with them, giving Bennett the opportunity to delay answering her as they rode to his floor in silence.

They entered the condo, and Bennett released Spike from his leash, hanging it by the door.

"I can't answer your earlier question without stating the obvious," Bennett began. "Selena told you about Delaney."

"Whew, I'm glad you brought up the emotional elephant in the room. I wasn't sure how to." Naomi sipped the water. "Yes, she felt bad, though. She assumed you'd told me."

"It's all right." Bennett took a swig from the bottle, then replaced the cap.

"She didn't give me any details. Only that Delaney was involved with drugs, and you ended up arresting her."

"I'd spent months building this case against a group of drug runners moving product in and out of Colorado." Bennett sighed and kicked his feet up on the coffee table. "I'd worked long hours, which means lack of sleep and unavailability to Delaney, both emotionally and physically. She seemed understanding and I assumed she accepted the sacrifice we'd both have to pay for my job." He snorted. "Imagine when I learned her 'understanding'—" Bennett made air quotes with his fingers "—was solely because she was working me for information to elude capture."

"How so?" Naomi didn't hide her confusion. "If you didn't see each other often, how was Delaney cognizant of where you were or what you were doing?"

"Whenever we got the opportunity to talk, she'd ask about case updates. Of course, I was thrilled she was interested."

"Isn't that a violation?"

"No, I didn't give her any classified details. Cops talk to their significant others. It's healthy to vent to someone safe," Bennett explained. "My captain had always taught us to include our spouses."

"I guess that makes sense." Naomi crossed her ankles, shifting on the sofa. "She was collecting information." Betraying Bennett's confidence and trust. No wonder he was bitter.

"Yes."

"What happened at the end?"

"I worked a straight seventy-two-hour shift, so I hadn't spoken to her during that time. One of our investigators got a lead, and we were closing in. Imagine my surprise when we busted inside for the takedown, and I found Delaney there with hundreds of pounds of cocaine."

Naomi leaned forward. "How awful." She understood the

pain of betrayal now like never before, and an unspoken compassion passed between her and Bennett. "I'm sad she did that to you."

"Yeah, you totally get it, huh?" Bennett's tone was soft. "I'm sorry for both of us."

"Based on what Selena told me yesterday, I'm sorry for all of us," Naomi added. "There are lots of happy marriages and families as proof that's not the norm."

"And there are as many torn apart by divorce," Bennett contended.

Naomi looked down. "Selena said our past experience helps us to make wiser choices for the future."

"As true as that might be, I cannot see myself ever going down that relationship road again." Bennett frowned. "I gave up a lot. Sacrificed too much. Had the chance to do more in my career, which I passed on because I wanted to be there for my wife and kids." He snorted. "Won't make that mistake again. I don't trust people, period."

"That's not true," Naomi said, lifting her chin. "You trust Selena and Spike." At the mention of his name, the beagle hopped onto the couch and lay beside her.

Bennett frowned but didn't refute her argument. "Spike's incapable of deception."

"Okay, fair enough, but what about your team and your co-workers at the Denver PD?"

"They've proven themselves."

"Isn't that accurate of most relationships? We learn more about one another as we spend time together. Considering you were going to arrest me for being a serial killer when we first met, look how far we've come," she teased.

That got a smile out of him. "True that."

"Which proves that not everyone is unworthy of your trust. And you're saying you can't imagine that happening if you fell in love?"

"I won't put myself into a position to find out." Bennett's

hardened tone and narrowed eyes stung Naomi. "Romance is out for me. I'd better get to work." Bennett rose and walked to his bedroom, closing the door softly behind him.

Naomi fidgeted with a string on her leggings. What possible rebuttal could she offer?

Selena had spoken truthfully.

Bennett wasn't a family man.

If only her heart accepted that reality.

Bennett immersed himself in the investigation, scouring the lists of recent murders in the surrounding states. There had to be a lead buried that they hadn't yet discovered. Working on the RMK and Ted's case simultaneously provided him a break from the uncomfortable and probing conversation with Naomi. She'd spent the morning busying herself rearranging tours with her contact, Addy, allowing him time alone to overthink.

He'd enjoyed their talk until they got stuck on discussing families and marriage. All that did was remind him of the things he'd never have.

Naomi was correct. Bennett trusted his teammates and coworkers, but after Delaney, he'd never offer that to another woman. He owed Delaney some gratitude. She'd awakened him to his lack of cop sense and how easily he'd set aside his skeptical nature for the sake of love. The risk had nearly cost his career and had taken a sizeable chunk of his self-esteem. A cost he wouldn't pay again.

The hurt and deflation of Naomi's enthusiasm had tugged at his heart while simultaneously activating his callous walls of self-protection. She hadn't pressed him, which made Bennett want to divulge his longing to trust her. At least he'd opened the door for that, until he'd chickened out before he spoke the words. Because as beautiful, sweet and fun as Naomi was to be around, she had the very real potential to break his heart.

A constant emotional tug of war had battled within him until he spotted the spark of hope in Naomi's eyes when they talked about relationships. He would not lead her on. That was far crueler. His harsh but firm replies squashed any erroneous ideas she might have about him. Hurting her wasn't his goal, but the alternative was telling her the truth.

He'd fallen hard for Naomi.

She'd endured hardship and betrayal, and Bennett refused to add to her pain by offering her hope. As excruciating as speaking the words were, it was for his own benefit as much as hers. His effort at stonewalling his heart required him to replay Delaney's treachery on an endless reel.

Naomi glanced up from where she sat talking to Spike, who lavished affection on her.

She was beautiful inside and out, and being around her would be his undoing.

He had to take down Roderick Jones and find the RMK so their time together would end. The reality of parting ways with Naomi saddened Bennett. Being without her sounded like a miserable life.

A text from Chase dragged Bennett from his ruminations. Video meeting now.

"Naomi, I have to take this conference call with my team."

She nodded mutely. With the hurt still evident on her face, everything within him wanted to comfort her, to tell her he was falling for her. Instead, he excused himself and went to his bedroom, closing the door behind him.

He logged in to the meeting. As his team members popped onto the screen, he replayed Naomi's comment about trusting them. To be fair, the trust occurred a little at a time. It wasn't instantaneous. When Chase had first recruited Bennett, he'd kept a distance until he'd verified their credibility. Was it possible to have that same emotion toward Naomi?

"Thanks for showing up on such short notice," Chase said, opening the meeting and commanding Bennett's attention. "Let's do a status check. Starting with Bennett."

"Selena already updated you all on the incident in the mountains. I doubt we'll ever find who attacked me, and all we have is the picture of Ted's note to go on."

"Yes, but we've got a solid connection to Roderick Jones," Selena added.

"He'll rear his ugly mug soon enough," Kyle replied. "He's behind the attacks on Naomi."

"I've requested DPD to keep the discovery on the down-low as much as possible, but Jones has deadbeats everywhere," Bennett explained. "By now, he's probably aware we confiscated the drugs from her van."

"But we believe there are more drugs?" Ashley asked.

"There must be. The money was significant, but it's not enough to get Jones's attention. There's something more he wants, and for whatever reason, he believes Naomi has it. That keeps her in danger," Bennett replied. "We need Jones to crawl out from under his rock, which his determination to get the stash provides."

"As a precaution, Kyle and I are assisting with Naomi's security detail," Selena said.

"Good work," Chase commented. "However, I'm stating the obvious here. That cannot continue indefinitely. If we don't get a lead on Jones soon, we'll have to surrender Naomi to another jurisdiction and focus on the Rocky Mountain Killer."

The order was a kick to the gut for Bennett. He couldn't pass Naomi off to just anyone. Determination fueled him to bring down Jones, and fast.

Chase continued, "We have no news on Cowgirl. The motive remains a mystery, although there are plenty of theories simmering down to a jerk who steals people's dogs." He sighed. "At this time, we do not believe her dognapping or missing status is a personal vendetta against our team."

"Could be a criminal backyard breeder," Bennett said, a sick feeling in his stomach at the thought.

"Let's hope not," Hannah said.

"Where are we with the RMK investigation?" Chase asked.

"We're still scouring the lists Isla provided, but thus far, we have nothing on any of the victims' enemies," Ashley reported. "Not to mention, with all the fights they were involved with and instigated, multiple incidents of cheating on their girlfriends, etcetera, they accumulated a lengthy list of haters."

"Kyle and I are headed back to Bennett's to do the same," Selena added. "We're also comparing the lab results from both the Montana and Colorado crime scenes."

"Currently, it's not much," Kyle said. "We also have no leads on the shooters from Bennett and Naomi's most recent attack. We found the truck—stolen of course—and the perps ditched it on a rural highway."

"We're spinning our wheels, people," Chase grumbled. "What're we missing?"

"The RMK is from Elk Valley or has a personal connection there," Isla said.

"The RMK was involved with or has some attachment to the Young Ranchers Club, which means, more than likely, they were from Elk Valley, too, and attended Elk Valley High School," Bennett added.

"Let's scour the yearbook and YRC enrollments," Rocco offered. Like Ashley, the cop had attended high school in Elk Valley at the time of the murders…it was a good idea.

Meadow said, "Bennett, maybe Naomi will have some input to help us?"

"I'll ask her."

"Excellent," Chase commended.

"I'll upload the electronic files to the shared folder," Isla advised, referencing the online system that housed the team's working documents.

"Update the team with all potential leads," Chase said.

"Naomi asked about accessing her apartment," Bennett explained. "Denver PD released the scene, but I contend she's not safe there until we apprehend Jones."

"Agreed. Selena and Kyle, please continue assisting in Naomi's security detail with Bennett," Chase ordered.

"Roger that," they replied.

Had he imagined the knowing look in Selena's gaze?

They disconnected, and Bennett returned to the living room to talk with Naomi.

His phone chimed with a text message from Isla, advising the files were ready. Bennett lifted his laptop and pulled up the documents. "Hey, Naomi. I need your help looking through the yearbook and YRC annuals for connections between the murder victims beyond what we already know."

"Sure."

He moved to sit beside her, not missing how she quickly scooted to the right and placed a pillow on her lap to hold. Her body language spoke clearly. Naomi had distanced herself from him.

And rightly so. He leaned back, sharing the laptop screen. "Let's start with the Young Ranchers Club."

He scrolled the pictures.

"It's hard to say," Naomi said. "We weren't a vast community, which means interacting with the same people every year. In a way, everyone is connected."

"That's what I was worried about." Bennett sighed.

THIRTEEN

Bennett's obnoxious ring tone jolted him awake. He glanced at the clock on his nightstand where the LED light flashed 05:30 a.m. Isla's contact information appeared on the screen, gaining his full attention. He swiped to answer, "Isla, what do you have for me?"

"Good morning to you, too," she jested. "I ran the concealed carry permit information, and discovered Ted Cavanaugh changed his name about ten years ago."

Why hadn't Eduardo picked up on that? No time for placing blame. "Any idea why?"

"Hang on, it gets better. Ted Cavanaugh, originally Theodore Pritchard, was born in North Platte, Nebraska. Orphaned at two years old and raised by his grandmother, Twila May Pritchard, née Cavanaugh, in Benser, Nebraska. She passed away right before Ted's nineteenth birthday."

"Naomi nailed it." Bennett sagged against the headboard. "He took her name out of respect."

"Hmm, but get this. Prior to the name change, police questioned him in eighteen-year-old Otto Lewis's missing person case."

Bennett sat up. "Why?"

"Apparently, Otto, Ted and Glen Kappel were friends. The local sheriff noted Otto and Ted were troublemakers, but weren't involved in criminal activities. By comparison, Glen had multiple arrests with a rap sheet ranging from theft to assault. He bounced from juvenile hall to jail numerous times. He was also questioned about Otto's disappearance."

"Where's Glen now?" Bennett asked.

"Hard to say. He doesn't have a bank account, credit cards or property. Tracking him hasn't proven easy."

"Were any of Glen's crimes related to narcotics?"

"His last arrest was for possession of meth in Big Springs, Nebraska, six years ago," Isla said. "He served two years, then was released on parole."

"Interesting."

"Was Otto found?"

"Nope. Investigation went cold."

"Without a body, they probably struggled to prove Otto was dead," Bennett thought aloud. "I wonder if the sheriff remembers anything about the case."

"It wouldn't hurt to ask. His name is Zechariah Motega. He retired five years ago."

"Got a LKA for me?" Bennett referenced the acronym for the last known address.

"Yes, Motega's a resident of the Pine Meadows Memory Assistance Retirement Home."

Bennett considered the information, then asked the inevitable question. "Alzheimer's?"

"Yes." Sadness hung in Isla's reply.

"Okay. What do we know about Otto?"

"His parents were less than desirable. They offered a weak justification for their inability to specify the date Otto had gone missing. All they claimed was he'd disappeared in early October." Isla grunted. "And I'm struggling to get approved as a foster parent."

"Gotta love the irony." Bennett blew out a long breath. "Ted Cavanaugh died in October, too."

"Yeah, I didn't consider that a coincidence, either," Isla said. "There was no evidence to indicate Theodore, aka Ted, or Glen were involved in Otto's disappearance other than the trio were friends."

"Except it's interesting Ted changed his name shortly thereafter and moved to Denver," Bennett replied. "Not to mention, he lied to Naomi, claiming he grew up in Colorado."

"Definitely suspicious."

"Outstanding work." Bennett leaned forward, wheels turning. "What about LKAs for Glen, Otto and Twila May?"

"Already sent it to your phone. Along with pictures of them."

Even as she said the words, Bennett's cell phone pinged with a PDF file. "You're the best."

"Tell me something I don't know." Isla chuckled.

"Any word on the investigation of your foster approval? Or ideas who's making false accusations against you?"

"Not yet." Isla sighed. "I'm hoping to talk to Chase about it this afternoon."

"Holler if I can help."

"Will do."

They disconnected, and Bennett googled Otto's case, locating an old news story on the web. Other than the suspicious nature of his disappearance, there was no proof of foul play. His parents assumed he ran away. Both Glen and Ted claimed they had last spoken to him the day before they went fishing at Lake McConaughy in Ogallala, Nebraska.

Bennett threw off his covers, eager to talk to Naomi. He walked to the living room, debating whether to wake her. To his surprise, she sat on the couch watching an old sitcom with the volume turned down. "I'm sorry. Was I too loud?"

"Not at all." He dropped onto the recliner. "I just got off the phone with Isla and have something I wanted to run past you."

"By the tone of your voice, it doesn't sound like good news." Naomi shut off the TV and faced him.

"Why are you up this early?"

"Bathroom break and I couldn't fall back asleep." She tilted her head. "What's up?"

"Just to clarify, Ted told you he'd grown up in Colorado?"

"Yes, in Denver. Why?"

"Apparently, that's untrue."

"Look at my shocked and amazed face," she deadpanned.

"He grew up in a small town near North Platte, Nebraska, called Benser, where he lived with his grandmother, Twila May Cavanaugh. Did he talk about his parents?"

"No, only that they died when he was young. He spoke of wanting to be a better father to our baby, since he'd never had one. Why are you asking all of this?"

"Were you aware Ted's birth name is Theodore Pritchard?"

Naomi blinked. "He lied to me about his name, too?"

"Technically, no." Spike strolled over to Bennett and hopped on his lap. "He legally changed his name to Ted Cavanaugh, taking Twila's maiden name."

"How negligent of me not to ask, 'Do you have any other identities,' when we were dating," she mumbled sarcastically.

"You're starting to sound like me," Bennett teased.

"I'm starting to appreciate why you feel the way you do."

Bennett grinned, though her words gave him a twinge of sadness. His pessimism had brought down the optimistic Naomi Carr-Cavanaugh.

"On second thought, perhaps after Twila's death, he changed his name to honor her?" she said.

There it was. Naomi thought the best of others. Even her deceitful husband.

"Possibly." Bennett prayed for wisdom. How much should he share with her?

"Is there more?" At his hesitation, she added, "After all we've been through, just tell me whatever it is you're trying hard to say nicely or not at all."

Bennett shared the information about Otto Lewis's disappearance, Glen Kappel and Ted's police questioning, and Glen's subsequent arrests for petty crimes. "Did Ted ever mention either man to you?"

"No. I've never heard of them." Naomi exhaled.

Bennett handed her his cell phone, displaying the pictures of the three men. She studied them, lingering on Ted's picture. Did she miss him? As if in response, she swiped back at Glen's mugshot taken from his last arrest. "Now that you mention it, there's something familiar about him."

"Did he come to your house?" Bennett leaned closer. "Hang out with Ted?"

"No." Naomi reviewed the phone. "I'll keep pondering, though. Were Glen and Ted suspected of Otto's disappearance?"

"Possibly. Otto's body was never found. I'd like to take a road trip to Nebraska and do a little checking for myself. Hoping to talk to the sheriff who handled the case. I'll ask Selena and Kyle to come here—"

"No way!" Naomi jumped up. "I'm tired of sitting on the sidelines. I'm going with you."

"Your doctor won't approve."

"Then don't tell her." She offered him a wan smile.

"Naomi." A warning hung in his voice. "This isn't a good idea."

"Bennett, I want to understand why the man I loved lied to me. If visiting his hometown will explain that, I'm tagging along. How much more stress is involved in riding in a car as opposed to waiting here?"

Bennett sighed. "I won't get approval to take you with me."

"Then ask for forgiveness when we return." She winked. "When do we leave?"

He got to his feet. "Twenty minutes. I'll shower quick first, and you must eat a healthy breakfast. It's a five-hour commute, which puts us at the state border around eleven o'clock."

Against the voice in his head warning against taking Naomi, Bennett gathered supplies for a road trip. Chase had said without leads on Roderick Jones, they'd assign Naomi's detail to someone else. Bennett reasoned he had no time to waste.

He sent a text to Selena and Kyle. Following up on a possible lead. Will be in touch.

Selena responded immediately. Need us to stay with Naomi?

He replied, Not yet. Then he prayed he wasn't making the biggest mistake of his career by taking her with him.

What skeletons did Ted Cavanaugh have hidden in Nebraska?

"Is it strange that I'm grateful those thugs attacked me at Peter's ranch?" The drive to Nebraska offered Naomi plenty of time to think.

Bennett flicked a glance her way. "Dare I ask why?"

"How else would I have discovered these things about Ted? Maybe it's part of helping me to let go. Not just of the dream of what I thought we had and lost, but to allow me a fresh start. I could've died without knowing why. Although ignorance is bliss." A truer statement could not be made. "I'm compelled to understand why Ted kept his background a secret."

"Agreed. And is the person after you actually Ted's enemy?"

"As in, something triggered that individual to want to kill me?"

"Yes." Bennett remained quiet for several minutes, then said, "You continually amaze me. What other person views the assaults you've encountered as God working in your life?"

"God is always active in our lives. Recognizing it is the key."

"You're the kind of person I want to be when I grow up," he quipped.

She giggled and swatted playfully at him. "Whatever."

"Now that we are armed with this information, which, for the record, could turn out to be absolutely nothing at all—"

"Or essential to the case," she interrupted.

Bennett chuckled. "I wonder what secrets Ted's enemy has on him."

"Yeah, and why now?"

"I'm hoping that talking to Sheriff Motega will answer that."

"If he's an advanced Alzheimer's patient, do you think he'll remember anything?" Naomi asked.

"Good question. He doesn't have living relatives, and the electronic case file Isla sent me was basically useless."

"I guess it takes the term *long shot* to a whole new level," Naomi said. "Any word on when you'll get your pickup back?"

"Not yet. I kind of like this sedan. Cheaper on gas," he kidded.

They'd driven through the Sand Hills, where rolling land spanned acres in all directions. "This is actually pretty."

"It's a huge contrast to Denver."

"Hmm. Maybe that's why Ted chose to move there."

The GPS automated voice advised Bennett to take a right from the highway into North Platte. He continued to the Pine Meadows Memory Assistance Retirement Home. A duck pond and blooming trees enhanced the serenity of the single-level facility.

He parked, and they exited the vehicle. Bennett leashed Spike with his official harness, which had the MCK9 logo, and they made their way to the front doors.

"Are they going to give us a hard time since we're not family?" Naomi asked.

"Isla called ahead and got us clearance with the director."

Bennett approached the young woman behind the reception desk and offered their names. She confirmed they were approved. After buzzing them through the doors, a nurse led them to a sunroom. One entire wall comprised of glass contained the biggest aviary cage Naomi had ever seen. Birds of every color, shape and size fluttered around inside.

A husky man with snow-white hair sat at a table fixated on the scene.

"Mr. Motega, you have guests," the nurse said as they strolled toward him.

Motega turned, spotting Spike. A wide smile spread across

his weathered face. "Poochy!" He reached out a hand, and Spike glanced at Bennett as though seeking permission.

"Be nice," Bennett said, kneeling beside the beagle.

Spike sniffed the older man's outstretched hand, then offered a lick of approval.

"You remember me, Poochy!" Sheriff Motega exclaimed.

Bennett and Naomi exchange worried glances. This might not pan out after all.

Naomi had enjoyed her time working with hospice patients, and her training returned. "Hello, Sheriff Motega," she said, intentionally using his title.

He glanced up, and awareness swept over his expression. "Hello, young lady. Have we met?" He patted his leg.

Bennett gave Spike a nod, and he hopped into Motega's lap, earning him a soft stroke of the head.

"No, sir. My name is Naomi—" she began.

"Like the woman in the Bible?" he asked, intrigued.

"Yes, sir."

"That's how my mother named me, too." He smiled.

"Sheriff, could Naomi and I talk with you about an old case of yours?" Bennett asked cautiously.

"Who're you?" Motega surveyed Bennett warily.

"Detective Bennett Ford, sir."

"Ah, a fellow lawman. All righty, have a seat." He gestured toward the chairs across from him.

Bennett quickly dragged the seats closer, then assisted Naomi into one before sitting beside her.

Naomi took the lead. "Sheriff, we are looking into the Otto Lewis case."

Motega's blank expression worried her.

After several seconds, he looked past them toward the birds, still absently petting Spike, who sat patiently, receiving the kind affection.

"Good boy, Spike," Bennett whispered.

"Birds should fly free. Not live in cages," Motega said. "Otto must have wanted to be free."

Naomi and Bennett shared a look. Neither was willing to interrupt the sheriff's moment of clarity.

"Never found him," he concluded.

"Sir, your notes mentioned little regarding your questioning of Otto's friends, Theodore Pritchard and Glen Kappel."

Motega's gaze slowly traversed to Naomi. "You a first-time mama?"

"Yes, sir." She placed her hands on her belly. "I can't wait to meet my baby boy."

"Boys." Motega snorted. "They keep secrets."

"Did Glen and Theodore keep secrets?" Bennett pressed.

Motega shook his head. "Hoodlums." His gaze reverted to the aviary, and he mumbled, "Poochy, critters don't wanna be caged. Like me."

Naomi's heartstrings tugged at the man's quiet confession. She looked around the room. Though pleasant and well maintained, the man before her no doubt missed his independence. Here, they monitored him constantly for safety reasons.

"Sir, can you tell us anything about Otto, Glen or Theodore?" Bennett pressed.

Naomi shook her head. Pushing Motega wouldn't help. Patience was the key.

"What's that funny vest you're wearing, Poochy?" Motega ignored Bennett.

"It's his uniform," Naomi explained. "He finds narcotics."

Motega looked up at her, wonderment in his eyes. "He learned to do that?" He smiled at the beagle. "And all that time, I thought you could only fetch slippers." He chuckled.

Bennett's expression fell.

Naomi wanted to assure him not to give up, but not at the risk of interrupting the moment. "Yes," she continued. "He helps Detective Ford."

Motega nodded, glancing at Bennett. "The factory."

"Beg your pardon," Bennett asked.

"They closed the old dairy factory outside of town." Motega shook his head. "Shoulda tore it down instead. Like everything in Benser, they abandoned it."

The nurse approached. "I'm sorry, but Mr. Motega needs to rest now."

Bennett sighed. "We understand."

"Thank you, sir." Naomi placed her hand over Motega's. "I enjoyed talking with you."

"Well, hello there." He met her gaze. "What's your name?"

The nurse offered her a supportive nod.

"My name is Naomi, Sheriff."

"Like in the Bible." He smiled.

"Yes, sir."

Bennett rose. "Come on, Spike, time to go."

The dog offered Motega another minute before hopping down.

"Thank you," Bennett addressed both the nurse and the sheriff.

Naomi led the way out of the facility.

"Well, that was a waste," Bennett groused.

"Are you kidding?" Naomi responded, sliding into the passenger seat. "He told us where to look."

Bennett loaded Spike and slid behind the wheel. "The factory?"

"Yes."

"He was confused, though. Rambling."

"At times, but the factory connected to a memory."

Bennett scanned his phone for any abandoned buildings that might fit the criteria. "There's one on the other side of Benser. I'd like to check out Twila May's house, too."

"Sounds good to me."

He started the engine. "Are you doing all right?"

"Yes. I forgot how much I enjoyed talking with patients. Maybe I'll get my nursing degree?"

"Really?"

"It's not as if I have a tour company anymore." She grunted.

"You do. It's just on a temporary hiatus."

"Right."

Bennett drove out of North Platte and headed northeast. Again, they traversed the Sand Hills until, out of nowhere, a smattering of brick buildings appeared in the distance. A run-down sign covered by vines and weeds, neglected and forgotten, advertised Welcome to Benser. A few small storefronts lined the main thoroughfare, and a gas station sat on the edge of town.

"Guess Benser isn't the local hot spot," Bennett quipped.

Following the GPS directions, they traveled to the address Isla had provided as Twila May's last known residence.

"Ted didn't talk a lot about growing up, but when he talked about his grandmother, he lit up," Naomi reminisced. She prayed his adoration for her was the sole reason for his name change.

A long, winding road led to the deserted property where weeds and trees swarmed the tiny house in overgrowth.

"Not sure what I thought we might find here," Bennett said, leaning forward to look out the window, "but this wasn't it."

"Didn't Isla already tell you it was abandoned?"

"Yes, but I hoped it wasn't in this bad of shape."

"Why not just tear it down?" Naomi asked. "It would be kinder than leaving the structure to slowly cave in on itself."

They pulled up to the broken chain-link fence gate and stopped. "There's no way you're going inside that dilapidated house."

"No argument here."

"Let's check out the factory."

Spike yawned, emitting a squeak as he stretched out on the seat beside her.

They drove ten miles east of Benser. The massive brick-and-iron structure stood amid the immense overgrowth of weeds and foliage. Bennett parked as close as possible to the building.

The factory had two floors, and multiple windows were missing or broken out. A tall steel cylinder protruded into the sky from one side and an old pipe lay in the parking lot—strange and out of place, yet simultaneously fitting with the scene.

Naomi scanned the area. "Do you hear horror music playing in the background?" she jested.

"A little bit," Bennett teased, shifting into Park. He withdrew his gun, checking the magazine. "You wait here. It's not safe."

"Are you kidding? That's right out of a slasher movie. You leave, and I'm sitting here alone when the killer finds me." Naomi shook her head. "No way. I'm going with you."

Bennett chuckled. "All righty then."

They exited the sedan, and Bennett passed Naomi a large flashlight. They slowly approached the structure, walking up the long cement loading dock. No doors restricted their access. Naomi flicked on the light and swept the beam through the room. Graffiti covered every wall, and a combination of atrocious smells assailed her senses. Bottles, cans and trash littered the floor of the main level.

"I can picture this as a teen hangout," Naomi said.

"Yeah, unfortunately, it provides ample space for nefarious acts." He kept Spike tucked under one arm as their feet crunched on broken glass. "Maybe that's what triggered Motega's memory of it. You talked about Spike searching for narcotics. This dump could've been used for drug deals."

"I hadn't thought of that. Otherwise, what did this place have to do with Motega's investigation?"

"Ted and Glen both claimed to be fishing when Otto went missing," Bennett said.

They moved cautiously through the room to the stairs at the far side.

"Dare we check out the upper level?"

"Stay close to me in case the floorboards aren't strong enough."

Naomi swept the beam overhead, illuminating the ceiling still intact.

Bennett placed Spike on the ground and activated a flashlight connected to his gun. Together, they slowly ascended the steel staircase to the second floor, then inched to the center of the room. They stopped, surveying the space where old dust-and-cobweb covered machines and furniture filled the space.

Naomi stepped forward and felt the board shift slightly beneath her feet. She quickly retreated. "That's unsafe."

Bennett looked down and gently helped her to move closer to the wall.

"What was this place?"

"Some kind of clothing or material factory," Bennett said.

Naomi rubbed her arms to ward off the chill that had nothing to do with the temperature.

"I told you they'd show up."

Naomi and Bennett spun to see two figures looming in the shadows behind them. The man's voice was familiar. As the duo—male and female—closed the distance, both wielding guns, she recognized the intruder who had threatened her at the hospital. The woman was also familiar, but Naomi couldn't place her. She opened her mouth to speak, but no sound came out. She had to warn Bennett. *God help us*.

"Put down the gun, cop."

Spike barked and growled, taking his guarding stance in front of Bennett and Naomi.

"Let me kill the dog," the woman said, staying in the shadows.

"Shut up, Hetti!" the man barked.

Awareness flitted over Bennett's face. "Hazel."

Naomi recalled his strange question about Hazel Houston.

"That's my alter ego when riding your tour bus, darlin'.

I'm Hetti Miller." The woman chuckled, stepping closer into the light.

"I saw you." The same person Naomi had spotted on several occasions around Bennett's condo.

"Duh. I watched you." She aimed her gun at Spike, still growling.

"Spike." Bennett silenced the beagle, who remained on guard.

"Put down the gun," the man repeated.

"Can't do that." Bennett replied, slowly moving toward Naomi. "Get behind me," he whispered.

Naomi started to move, and the woman fired, striking the floor in front of her.

"Don't you dare," the woman ordered.

Naomi gasped and froze.

"Hello, Glen," Bennett said, tone steely.

"Do what you're told, or we'll shoot all of you." The man stepped closer, where sunlight streamed through the broken windows, illuminating his face and the familiar scar over his left eyebrow.

Realization slammed into her. The mugshot Bennett had shown her of Glen was a younger and thinner version. "That's why he looked familiar to me! He's the guy who threatened me at the hospital," Naomi gasped, finally finding her voice.

"I'm touched you remember me." Glen cackled. "Would've saved a lot of trouble if that stupid nurse hadn't interrupted us."

"Was Nolice working with you?" Bennett asked.

Glen tilted his head, clearly confused. "Who?"

"Stop wasting time!" the woman fired again, nearly hitting Spike. "Drop the gun!"

"Enough!" Bennett's jaw tightened as he lowered his gun to the ground.

"Kick it away from you!" Glen ordered.

Bennett complied. "Why did you kill Ted, Glen?"

"It was an accident," Hetti replied in defense.

"No. Ted did it to himself. He told you everything. Didn't he, Naomi?" Glen addressed Naomi, slurring his words.

Great. He was intoxicated. And armed. Not a good combination.

Naomi took a half step to the right, feeling the weight of the board shift under her. She hesitated. The same place she'd warned Bennett about. Death by gunshot wounds or falling through the floor? Neither sounded appealing.

"Until this morning, I'd never heard of you, Glen," Naomi said.

"As if I'd buy that," Glen growled. He fired into the rafters, and a cloud of dust rained down on them. "Gimme my drugs!"

"Boards are weak," Naomi whispered.

Bennett gave her an almost imperceptible nod. "You mean Roderick Jones's drugs."

Glen glowered at them. "Where are they?"

"Tell him!" Hetti hollered. "Roderick will kill Glen! Don't you understand?"

"Shut up, Hetti!" Glen barked.

"Ted lied to me," Naomi said.

"No. He told you," Glen insisted. "Now, I'll ask once more. Where are the drugs?"

"They're in police custody," Bennett responded.

"Some, but not the big stash," Glen argued. "Give me them, and I'll let you go. I've protected you, Naomi. You owe me."

She blinked, confused.

"Do it!" Hetti screeched.

Glen glared at her. "I'll shoot you myself if you don't keep quiet!"

Hetti cowered.

"I… I don't know," Naomi stammered. Visions of the assault at Peter's ranch fluttering around her in the repeated scene.

"Why else are you here?" Glen challenged. "You just happened to show up at this decrepit factory? Of all the places in the world? Ted told you about everything! Including Otto!"

"Where is Otto?" Bennett said.

"Ted was such a wimp. Whining about confession and judgment before his kid was born. It's too late. You can't fix everything with the truth!" Glen threw back his head and hollered. "That was our secret! I covered Ted. He's the reason Otto died! But I helped Ted. He never would've survived prison. So, you owe me now, too, Naomi. For your husband's betrayal."

She'd use the illusion of them sharing a common enemy. "He betrayed us both," Naomi said.

A cackling ringtone filled the cavernous space. Glen withdrew his phone with one hand, keeping his gun trained on them, and answered, "Yeah. I'm getting it. Yes. I'll have it today." He slid the device into his pocket and swallowed hard enough that Naomi could see his Adam's apple bob. "Time is running out for us. If you want to live, speak."

"It's over, Naomi," Bennett said. "I'll take you where Ted hid your stash. Look, Spike is a narcotics dog." He gestured to the beagle. "He can help."

Naomi blinked. What was Bennett doing?

He lifted his hands in surrender. "C'mon. I'll go with you."

"No way," Glen argued. "Just tell me."

"Thing is, we're not positive. It's somewhere on Twila's land."

Glen seemed to consider the news. "Then I don't need you." He aimed the gun.

"Except you'll be digging for days looking, right?" Bennett said. "But with him, we'll find it fast."

"Then gimme your dog."

"Can't, dude." Bennett shook his head. "He'll only obey me. Just one condition. Let Naomi go."

"Okay, you and the mutt come with me." Glen paused. "Hetti, you keep Naomi here." He waved Bennett closer with the gun. "She's insurance. If the cop's lying, kill her."

"You got it, honey," Hetti replied.

Bennett stepped in front of Naomi, surreptitiously passing her Spike's leash. He held up his hands. "I'm unarmed. See?"

Naomi kept the leash low, out of sight.

Bennett now shielded her with his body.

Spike stood at her feet, whining.

He took two more stalking steps, closing the distance between himself and Glen. "We'll get the drugs and come right back," Bennett cooed.

Then, like a flash, Bennett's arm swung out and swatted the gun from Glen's unsuspecting hand. The pistol toppled to the floor.

Hetti screamed.

Glen lunged for Bennett, tackling him. They rolled in a flurry of fists and kicks.

Naomi tugged Spike closer to her and moved against the wall.

Hetti lifted her weapon, meeting Naomi's eyes. "If Roderick doesn't get those drugs back, you will die tonight."

Bennett and Glen wrestled, rolling too close to the weakened floorboards.

Then a loud crack as the wood gave way.

Hetti and Naomi screamed.

FOURTEEN

Bennett rolled away from the gaping hole in the floorboard and peered down to where Glen's lifeless body lay below.

Hetti screamed and rushed to the hole, falling to her knees.

Naomi stood frozen, Spike at her side.

Bennett wasted no time. He jumped to his feet and jerked the pistol from the weeping woman. "Hetti Miller, you're under arrest." He helped her to kneel, kept her hands behind her back and snapped on flexicuffs. "Stay here."

"Glen!" she cried. "Get help!"

"I'll call for an ambulance," Bennett assured her. "Naomi, take away her gun and keep an eye on her while I check on Glen."

The fight withered from Hetti. Her head hung as she cried and repeated, "Roderick is going to kill us. We must find the drugs."

Naomi held the woman at gunpoint, still looking unsure about it.

"I'll be right back. Spike, stay. Guard."

The beagle took his stance in front of Naomi.

Bennett rushed to the main level, calling for backup as he approached Glen's body. He checked his neck, confirming there was no pulse. Then hurried up to the second floor, where Hetti still rambled and bawled.

Naomi passed Hetti's gun to Bennett, and he helped her to sit against the wall. Bennett called Chase and offered a speedy synopsis, promising he'd update the team with a full report ASAP.

His commander was clearly unhappy, but agreed they'd discuss it later.

Naomi huddled close to Bennett as Spike sniffed the area.

"Spike, stay over here," Bennett ordered, tugging the leash to prevent the beagle from falling through the rotted floor.

"Hetti, this is your opportunity to confess."

The woman sniffled and looked up, mascara streaming in long black rivers down her face. "Ted hid the drugs. Glen knew Ted told you." She jerked a chin toward Naomi.

"He didn't," Naomi assured her.

Hetti blinked as though seeing her for the first time. "But you said—" she addressed Bennett "—you'd take Glen."

He shook his head.

"You protected her." Hetti's gaze bounced between Bennett and Naomi.

"Yes." Bennett folded his arms. "What happened to Otto? What did Glen mean when he said Ted killed Otto?"

"If I tell you—" Hetti lifted her chin "—I want immunity."

"I can't make that agreement, but I'll tell the prosecutor how you complied."

She sighed with resignation. "It was a game. Ted, Otto and Glen were all drinking and hanging out here. Ted dared Otto to walk the rafters." Hetti jerked a chin toward the ceiling.

Long steel beams ran the full length of the building, spaced about two feet apart.

"Otto fell and broke his neck," Hetti said softly. "Just like Glen." She gazed at the hole in the floor.

"Where did they put Otto's body?" Bennett asked.

"They buried him on Ted's grandmother's property."

Spike sniffed where the dust from the rafters littered the floor. Bennett recognized the dog's attentiveness. "Spike. Find the cookies!"

The beagle's white-tipped tail wagged, and he continued circling the area. He barked twice. Paused. Barked twice again. Bennett illuminated his flashlight and swept the beam overhead, spotting the package sticking out from the side of the rafter.

Naomi looked up. "Is that...?"

"Yep, there's Jones's drug stash. When Hetti shot at the ceiling, she must've hit the bag."

Hetti blinked. "It was here all along?"

The sound of sirens filled the atmosphere.

Nine hours later, Bennett sat in his bedroom, laptop perched on his thighs, updating the team.

"You can't make this stuff up," Selena said.

"Tell me about it. Hetti talked freely, though doubtful they'll offer any leniency in her sentence. She was fully cognizant of her actions."

"I'm astounded she stalked Naomi, riding along on her tours," Meadow replied.

"She and Glen assumed she'd find the drugs if she stuck with Naomi long enough," Bennett said. His cell phone rang. "It's the Nebraska State Patrol."

He answered while his teammates watched from the other side of the screen.

"Detective Bennett, cadaver dogs located human remains at Twila May Cavanaugh's property," the NSP trooper advised. "We'll get DNA confirmation but looks like it's Otto Lewis."

"Thank you." Bennett disconnected. "They found Otto."

A quiet silence hung over the group.

"At least his family will get closure," Rocco said.

"If Ted and Glen had gone to the police and told them Otto's death was an accident, it would've changed everything," Bennett said. "Instead, Glen talked Ted into hiding the body, using fear to make him complacent."

"And giving Glen something to lord over Ted, to control him later on," Kyle replied.

"Hetti said Glen got in deep with Jones while incarcerated," Bennett said. "He'd kept tabs on Ted over the years, ensuring their secret about Otto remained a secret."

"Then when Ted went to Glen looking for a way to make

fast money, Glen connected him with Jones," Selena surmised. "Hetti confirmed Ted hid Jones's stash, then buried the box before telling Glen he planned to confess everything to the cops." Bennett shook his head. "They fought at Beaver Brook Trail, and he shoved Ted off the cliff."

"He'd witnessed how twisted Glen was," Meadow chimed in.

"Definitely," Bennett replied.

"Naomi recognized Glen at the factory, but not from the pictures?" Rocco asked.

"Yeah. It wasn't a current photo. He'd aged and gained weight. He also didn't have the scar she'd focused on until his battle with Ted, so it wasn't in his mug shot," Bennett explained.

"Ted had fought for his life," Kyle surmised.

"Yes," Bennett said.

Ashley chimed in. "Glen was the one who attacked you and stole the box at Beaver Brook Trail?"

"Hetti said when he found it was empty, he was furious." Bennett wiped a hand over his head. "Jones pressured Glen. Even called him at the factory. Glen and Hetti followed us to Nebraska, assuming we went to retrieve the drugs. He planned to kill us as soon as he got them."

"Still no word on Roderick Jones's whereabouts," Chase grunted. "We've got APBs and BOLOs out." He referenced the "all points bulletin" and "be on the lookout" law enforcement notifications.

"He'll pop up somewhere," Hannah assured the team.

"The scripture Ted scrawled on the letter to Naomi was his confession. He wanted to make things right, but Glen got to him before he could," Bennett said. "Without Naomi's help talking to Sheriff Motega, I'd have never considered the factory." Bennett hoped Chase would lessen the disciplinary action he no doubt had planned for Bennett for taking Naomi into the situation.

"Yes, Naomi's been invaluable," Chase replied. "We'll discuss it further privately."

Selena offered a sympathetic glance.

Bennett should expect administrative leave. He sighed.

"We still have no updates on Cowgirl," Ashley said.

"Keep praying, people. On that note, please add Isla to your prayers," Chase replied. He'd updated the group on the foster approval situation earlier in the day.

"Thank you," Isla said.

"All right, team, get some rest." Chase prepared to end the meeting.

"Before we disconnect, Bennett, Kyle and I will wrap up here at the Windham Ranch and head your way," Selena added. "We'll swing through and grab takeout from that great little Mexican restaurant off Hampden Avenue."

"Outstanding," Bennett agreed. "I love that place."

"Not fair," Ashley whined with a teasing grin.

"It's the perks of living in Denver," Bennett shrugged. "Thanks, guys."

The group disconnected, and he closed his laptop, concern returning for poor Cowgirl. *Lord, please help us find her.* He struggled to accept that a loving and kind person would steal the dog but then treat her well. Bennett prayed it was true, because the alternatives made his stomach roil.

He exited his bedroom and padded to the living room. Naomi sat up at his approach, apprehension etched in her expression. "Everything okay?"

Bennett shrugged, dropping on the recliner. His cell phone rang before he answered Naomi. "Hey, Selena."

"Does Naomi have any aversions or cravings?"

"Selena and Kyle are picking up Mexican food for dinner," Bennett relayed to her. "Do you have any requests?"

A wide grin spread across Naomi's face. "Yes, please! A green chili smothered beef and bean burrito."

Bennett repeated the order.

"A girl after my own heart," Selena chuckled.

"Yeah, add two of those for me, too," he said.

"Got it. See you soon."

They disconnected, and Bennett slid his phone into his shirt pocket.

"There must be something to the power of suggestion," Naomi said. "I wasn't even hungry, and now I'm craving that burrito big-time."

"What a day." Bennett flopped into his recliner.

"I like law enforcement work," she teased.

"I'll notify the team you're interested," Bennett chuckled.

A chime from the bedroom got their attention.

"That's my cell phone."

"I'll get it." Bennett hurried to the spare room, retrieving the device and passing it to her.

She swiped at the screen. Her forehead creased and her brows lifted.

"What's up?"

She held it up for him to read the text message.

Naomi, go to the ER ASAP. Have results from bloodwork and found something. Meet you there.
Dr. P.

"Your doctor texts instead of calling you?" Bennett asked.

"Yes, she often communicates that way with me, especially if she's multitasking with deliveries at the hospital."

"Oh. I suppose that makes sense."

"What do you think it means?" Her lip quivered. "Bennett, is there a complication with the baby?" Her hands covered her belly protectively.

"Let's stay positive. Might be a simple low blood sugar issue." Though apprehension consumed his heart. Bennett checked the clock display on his cell phone. "The doctor's office is closed now. She wants to make sure we don't wait until morning." Even as he spoke the words, he realized how it sounded. What was urgent enough that it required her to go to the ER? "Let's not waste time second-guessing." He stead-ied his voice and inflection to keep her calm.

"You're right."

Bennett helped her to her feet, and she hurried to the spare bedroom to put on her shoes.

He glanced at Spike. He'd be fine alone for a little while, but if it took hours, Bennett didn't want to leave him unattended. He'd text Selena and Kyle on the way.

Bennett snapped on Spike's leash as Naomi returned to the living room. He gave her a sideways hug. "Don't let your imag-ination take you to dark places. It'll be all right." He prayed that was true. "Would you like me to bring the car to you?"

"No. I'd rather walk."

He started to argue with her but didn't want to add to her worries and stress, fearing that would be worse.

They hurried from the condo and down the elevator to the basement level. Bennett's rental car sat in his assigned spot at the far end of the garage. As usual, automobiles filled the other spaces.

As they neared the vehicle, Spike barked twice, paused and barked again.

Bennett hesitated, placing a hand on Naomi's arm to halt her. A large pillar stood between them and the vehicle.

He withdrew his gun, cautiously inching toward the cement structure, while motioning with his other hand for Naomi to follow him.

Bennett peered around the post.

A bullet pinged the cement beside his head.

"Naomi, down!" Bennett ducked and turned to look be-hind him.

He'd made a huge mistake.

Naomi didn't dare move or breathe. The man's arm snaked around her neck, constricting tighter, and nearly eliminated her oxygen supply. Her eyes pleaded with Bennett.

His dire expression added to her fears.

"Roderick Jones." Bennett practically growled the name.

Awareness pummeled Naomi. She hadn't seen her attacker before he'd taken her hostage.

Unable to speak, she focused on guarding her throat. Her hand clamped onto Jones's arm, creating a small gap to keep him from strangling her.

He tugged her backward, and she stumbled off-balance, dropping her hands to steady herself.

Familiar muscle pain tightened across her back and belly.

Please God, not again. Not now. The contractions had been sporadic all day, but they weren't coming at regular intervals. She'd timed them to be sure. Plus, they'd felt similar to the Braxton-Hicks ones she'd experienced before.

Naomi processed the implications. If she was in labor, the stress of Jones holding her hostage was adding to their intensity. The nurse had instructed her to take deep cleansing breaths to calm herself, but Jones's hold restricted Naomi's attempts to comply.

Spike continued barking and snapping from his leash, but Bennett kept him nearby.

A sardonic guffaw too close to her ear preempted the man's response. "Shut that dog up, or I'll silence him for good." He positioned the gun, ensuring the barrel sat directly in front of Naomi's face.

"No!" she cried, arms outstretched as though she could protect Spike.

Bennett quieted the beagle with a single tug on his leash.

Spike dropped to sit beside him. He laser-focused on Jones, emitting a low growl.

"She doesn't have what you're looking for."

"Of course not, because my drugs belong to the stinking Nebraska State Patrol." Jones jerked her harder, causing Naomi to flail her arms for balance and forcing her to lean back against the man's chest.

She cringed at touching him. "Then what do you want?" Naomi choked, stalling for time and trying to breathe. Somehow, she didn't think Jones would put a pause on holding her hostage so she could give birth. If he got her alone in a vehicle, she was dead for certain.

"You're kidding, right?" Jones snorted, speaking too loudly for their proximity. "You owe me. And you're going to pay."

"You used a texting app and sent her the message, making it appear as though her doctor sent it," Bennett said, clearly stalling as he moved in a stalking motion. He was searching for a way to shoot Jones without hitting her.

Naomi pieced together the details. Her number was plastered all over the side of her tour bus. Easy access for Jones.

"See? Too bad you didn't use that brilliant deduction skill before all of this." Jones laughed again. "That's how you cops are, right? Too little and too late, always behind in the chase. But I'll admit you got me this time. You found my drugs before that loser Glen did." He jerked harder on Naomi.

Stars danced before her eyes as the lack of oxygen started impeding her ability to function. Pain erupted through her back and belly. The contractions were coming on stronger.

"Since I lost all that important revenue, I'll make sure Naomi here pays sufficiently." His hot breath against her ear made her want to vomit.

Bennett worked his jaw, still holding his weapon steadily.

"Drop the gun, cop. Then get in your car with your dumb dog and wait until I give you further instructions." Jones's voice went up several decibels, rattling Naomi's brain. "Gimme a reason to kill her in front of you."

"You'll never get away with this. She's nine months pregnant. If she knew anything, she'd tell you to protect her baby."

Naomi swallowed hard against Jones's tight grip around her throat. *Lord, please somehow save my son.*

"Naomi's been in on the whole thing from the beginning."

Jones's sardonic laugh was like nails on a chalkboard. "She had you buffaloed, right? All innocent-acting."

A flash of what Naomi guessed was fury passed over Bennett's face. After all he'd endured, would he believe Jones? Her heart hurt at the thought. No, she loved Bennett. She'd never hurt him.

Lord, help me. How do I prove to Bennett that Jones is lying? She met Bennett's eyes, hoping with all her being that if she died today, he'd recognize Jones wasn't telling the truth. She'd never told Bennett that she'd fallen in love with him. But she couldn't bear for him to think she'd betrayed him.

As though understanding passed between them, Bennett's expression softened. "No. You're a liar. Naomi was never involved with Ted's crimes. She has nothing to offer you, so let her go."

Naomi squeezed her eyes shut. If this ended badly, at least he knew she hadn't lied to him.

"That's the difference between us. Revenge is sufficient for me." Jones tightened his hold until Naomi could barely breathe. "Put down the gun, cop. Now!" He fired a shot beside Spike. The beagle never wavered from his glowering stance.

Bennett's murderous stare didn't shift from Jones as he slowly placed the weapon on the ground. But as he glanced up, Naomi noticed a slight flicker in his eyes. She watched him for any signs or instructions. Did he have a plan?

Screeching tires had Jones jerking Naomi to the side.

She spotted Selena's familiar SUV as it barreled toward them.

Jones relaxed his hold slightly on Naomi's throat.

She took the opportunity and threw her elbow back, catching him under the ribs. He gasped.

Spike bounded toward them, barking and snarling just as Selena skidded to a halt in front of them.

Jones shoved Naomi to the side. She crashed into the door of a minivan parked to the left and caught herself before falling.

He lunged over Selena's hood, attempting to escape, and ran in the opposite direction.

Naomi ducked and scurried to hide behind the minivan.

A blur passed her. Bennett. He dove for his weapon and raised it. A single blast echoed in the cavernous garage.

Naomi peered around the quarter panel to see Jones stumbling, the back of his shirt already absorbing a crimson stain.

Bennett's bullet found its mark.

Jones spun and aimed. Barking erupted as Scout and Spike bolted straight for him. The man lowered the weapon, then turned to run. The dogs easily caught up with Jones, tackling him face down to the ground in a tag-team attack.

Jones hollered, swatting at the unrelenting K-9s. Scout clamped his jaws on Jones's gun-wielding hand. The man screamed, dropping the weapon.

"Stop moving, or the dogs will not let go!" Kyle shouted.

"Stop moving!" Selena repeated.

Jones relented and lay prostrate on the garage floor.

"Scout, Spike, release!" Selena said.

The Belgian Malinois immediately released hold of Jones's arm and slowly backed away. Spike gave one more warning growl, tugging on Jones's pants before releasing the fabric. He panted, satisfied beside his K-9 partner.

Kyle rushed forward and snapped cuffs onto Jones's wrists while Selena collected his gun.

Bennett closed in on them, keeping the drug dealer at gunpoint.

Jones cursed. "I'm injured. Call an ambulance, I'm going to die!"

"Nah, you'll just hurt for a while," Kyle replied, checking over the wound.

"Prison provides plenty of healing time," Selena added.

Kyle hoisted Jones to his feet while the man spewed curses.

"This isn't over!" Jones threatened.

"Oh, but it is," Bennett said. "Remember, we have you and

your drugs, and based on the amount, your supplier will be very upset."

Jones glared, then returned to hollering a few more choice words as Kyle placed him in the back seat of the SUV.

While Kyle and Selena dealt with Jones, Bennett spun and ran to Naomi, pulling her into his arms. "Are you okay?"

"Yes," she croaked against her sore throat. She clung to him, unable to let go. Spike hopped up, planting his paws against her thigh. She glanced down and smiled. "Thank you, Spike."

"I've got you. You're safe," Bennett whispered.

"You believed me."

"I might not have the best track record with trusting people, but my heart said you weren't involved with Ted's crimes." In Bennett's embrace, Naomi clung for life, allowing him to bear the weight of her relief, her fears and all that she'd endured since the start of Jones's terror. "I've got you." He pressed a kiss against her temple and Naomi closed her eyes, accepting his comforting hold.

"Are you okay to walk?" Bennett asked.

Naomi realized the contractions had slowed sometime during the chaos, proving they were Braxton-Hicks. She nodded.

Bennett placed a hand on the small of her back, supporting her arm as they walked toward Selena's SUV. Spike trotted happily beside them. "How'd you know where to find us?" Naomi asked, rubbing her throat.

"We had the windows rolled down. When we pulled into the garage, Jones's voice carried to us. Then we heard Spike barking, and it was apparent something was wrong," Selena explained.

If not for Bennett's powerful hold on her, Naomi was certain she'd crumble. Her body felt weak and achy all at once.

"Naomi?" Bennett asked, looking into her eyes.

"My." A cramp gripped her harder than anything she'd experienced before, tightening around her back and stomach like a giant hand. "Oh." She gasped, clinging to Bennett. A puddle beneath her indicated what she already knew. "My water just broke."

"What?"

"She's in labor!" Selena cried.

Wordlessly, Kyle took Bennett's keys and ran to the rental car. He returned within record time and jumped out, allowing Bennett to slide behind the wheel. Kyle helped Naomi into the front seat and snapped on her seat belt.

"We'll call the hospital and notify them you're on the way," Selena advised.

"Thank…you." Naomi gasped.

Kyle hoisted Spike into his arms, and Bennett drove from the garage.

"Breathe, breathe," Bennett said, concentrating on the windshield, his tone steady and calm.

"I guess that was the stress Dr. Pankratz warned us about," she joked, then sucked in a breath to get through the approaching pain wave.

Bennett pulled onto the street. "Yeah. Remind me to charge Jones with that, too," he retorted sarcastically. "Okay, tell me when the next one starts, and I'll time it."

Naomi tried to laugh, but another contraction took hold. "Now," she gasped, breathing through it. When it ended, she exhaled.

"Doing all right?"

"Yes," she said.

"The contractions came on suddenly?" he asked.

"Sorta. I've had them sporadically most of the day, but I didn't think much of it since they were in my back."

"Why didn't you tell me?"

She winced.

The drive to the hospital seemed to last for hours, though the dashboard clock testified to a twenty-minute commute. Bennett did a great job of remaining calm, and his presence helped Naomi.

When they reached the emergency entrance, Bennett parked the car under the ambulance awning, then rushed to help Naomi from the passenger seat. A nurse hurried toward them with a wheelchair, guiding Naomi into the building.

"Her contractions are steady at five minutes apart." Bennett provided a recap.

"Stay with me, please," Naomi pleaded, suddenly afraid to be alone.

"I will. I'm here."

"Park your car and meet us in L and D," the nurse ordered.

He nodded and scurried outside while the nurse guided Naomi's wheelchair to the Labor and Delivery Unit. There, the nursing team helped Naomi change into a birthing gown, then settled her into the bed. The contractions remained constant.

Bennett returned shortly thereafter, though Naomi lost track of time in the chaos.

"Please hand me my cell? I want to tell Evan."

"Sure."

He dug her phone out of her purse and passed it to Naomi. She unlocked the screen and opened the running thread of text messages with Evan.

You're about to become an uncle. Come to Rose Faith Hospital ASAP!

He responded within a few seconds. Congrats, can't wait to meet my little nephew. Be there in the morning. He'd even added a heart emoji.

Unable to contain her joy, Naomi's eyes welled with tears for her brother's support. No matter how many years, tragedies and miles separated them, Evan was still her big brother. Always there for her.

She glanced to her right where Bennett sat. She passed him her phone, and he held her hand as she breathed through another contraction. "This is the real deal."

FIFTEEN

Bennett sat in the waiting room, staring at the massive TV screen on the wall.

"Has Naomi delivered?"

He glanced up at the familiar voice. Addy Everett entered, clutching a stuffed bear. "How did you know she was here?" Something about the woman rubbed him wrong.

"She texted me."

Bennett quirked a brow, still guarded.

"I can show you if you don't believe me." Addy held out her phone. "I agreed to take her tours until she returns to work." She lifted one hand in surrender.

He hesitated, contemplating if Naomi's assessment of the woman was accurate.

"We didn't start off on a good foot or shoe—however that saying goes." Addy closed the distance between them, then sat in the chair opposite Bennett. "Naomi is a wonderful person. I'm glad she has someone looking out for her finally. She deserves to be happy."

Bennett blinked. "I think so, too." He relaxed a little. "The doctor is with her now."

"I have a tour in the morning, so I wanted to bring by a new agreement." She handed Bennett an envelope. "This is the list of tours I'm handling for her temporarily. We agreed on a split profit, but I changed it."

Bennett opened his mouth to defend Naomi.

"She'll get the entire profit. They were her customers to start."
Addy tossed him the toy. "I can't stay, but will you tell her?"

"Yes." Bennett balked, slightly taken aback. Had he totally
misread Addy?

"See ya." She stood and walked away without another word.

A strange person, but not unkind.

He dropped onto a chair, leg bouncing with the stuffed animal tucked under his arm.

The nurse handling Naomi's delivery approached.

He opened his mouth to ask about Naomi's status, but she
stopped him with her lifted palm. "She's progressing, but the
doctor's not quite finished with the exam."

He exhaled.

"I see tons of fathers-to-be, but I have to say, you're making me nervous," she laughed. "Go walk off some of that antsy
energy."

"You think there's time?" Bennett halted in place. "A short
one?"

"Babies arrive when they're good and ready and not a second before."

"Right." Having never been in this position before, he was
unsure where he was supposed to be during that time. Naomi
hadn't asked for him to witness or assist in the delivery, and
he didn't press. But he also hesitated to leave her, even for a
second. The threat of Jones hurting her was finally over. So
what was his compulsion?

"Get out of here. Grab a coffee. A candy bar. Something,"
she said, shooing him with one hand and a wink.

Had Naomi changed her mind? Maybe she didn't want him
in the room while she delivered? The look on the nurse's face
remained stoic. He took the hint and didn't press.

"Okay." Bennett strolled toward the stairs, opting to take
those instead of the elevator while his mind roamed wildly.

He cared for Naomi, and he wanted to tell her. What right
did he have to do that? What could he offer a wonderful woman

like Naomi Carr-Cavanaugh? He was broken and scarred. She deserved the best. Better than him.

Was that a cop-out? Probably. The truth was, Bennett feared getting hurt again.

Seeing Naomi vulnerable with Jones triggered him to save her and express his love. He'd never felt this way. Not even for Delaney.

This was the real thing.

And it terrified him.

Naomi had endured indescribable pain and obstacles, yet her faith remained strong. She didn't place what Ted had done on anyone other than him. How had she worded it? He owned his mistakes. They belonged to him, not those who came after him. The words struck him afresh as they had the first time. He was trying to make Delaney pay by putting himself in a prison of solidarity and shutting out everyone else in his future. She wasn't paying for hurting him; he was. The ridiculousness of it smacked Bennett.

His feet seemed to move on their own as his brain traversed the complicated relationship road. Before he realized it, he'd made his way outside to get some air. The moon was bright in the cloudless sky.

As he stood staring up, he accepted the truth. He wanted Naomi in his life and longed for a future with her and her sweet baby. Though he feared the risks, the idea of joyful holidays, and first everything like birthday parties and Christmases offered a newfound joy to his heart he'd never experienced.

He spun on his heel, then paused.

Though timing was essential.

She was busy now and needed to rest. But as soon as he could, he'd tell her. He wouldn't waste a single second. He would confess he'd fallen in love with her and wanted a future with her.

Bennett dropped onto a bench outside the hospital and texted Selena and Kyle for a status check.

Within a few minutes, their reply bounced through.

Dogs secure at Denver PD. J in jail. En route, ETA thirty.

Another message pinged through his cell phone with a task force text from Meadow.

UPDATE ON COWGIRL. I'm in Elk Valley at HQ. I spotted Cowgirl darting around in a restaurant alley for food earlier! I used food to lure and coax her, and although I got close, Cowgirl fled across the street, into the park and then into the woods. Still searching. Keep praying!

The group quickly responded with promises to continue praying for Cowgirl and a quick rescue return.

Bennett bowed his head to pray for Naomi and a safe delivery, for Cowgirl's safe rescue and for the courage to tell Naomi that he'd fallen for her. And for the first time, Bennett offered his hopes, dreams and future to God, trusting His plan. A peace he'd not experienced since before his days with Delaney swept over him.

Satisfied, he stood and strolled back to Naomi's room.

The door was ajar, so he rapped softly, then startled as a nurse peered out. "Perfect timing."

Bennett quirked a brow, unsure what she meant until he entered and found Naomi holding a tiny, blanketed bundle.

He gaped. "Was I gone that long?"

Naomi chuckled softly. "Nope, little man was just ready to make his appearance."

"Don't let her fool you," the nurse said. "She was a rock star. Made delivery look easy." She winked and exited.

"I don't know about that," Naomi whispered, brushing her lips over the infant's head. "Come and meet August Lee. I named him after my dad, but I think we'll call him Augie for short." She yawned, then glanced down at the baby, her long eyelashes shadowing her cheek. Even in her exhaustion, she'd never looked more lovely.

Bennett quickly moved to her side and studied the perfect baby with his soft skin and bright eyes, mesmerized by Naomi. Bennett smiled. "He's beautiful."

"Would you like to hold him?"

The offer to hold the most precious part of Naomi's heart overwhelmed Bennett. The ultimate level of trust. Emotion swelled within him. "Yes. Please."

Bennett gently took Augie from Naomi's arms, cradling the infant close to his chest. The baby's tiny hand emerged from the blanket, gripping Bennett's finger. Like a wave, protectiveness and the overwhelming urge to care for this little person overtook Bennett. Tears filled his eyes, but he dared not wipe them away for fear of not properly cradling the baby. "He's perfect," he croaked through his tight throat.

"Yes." Naomi's reply was soft and tender. She nestled down under the covers.

"Rest." Bennett slid into a chair beside her bed, still holding the tiny infant. "I'll be here when you wake." *And every single day hereafter. If you'll let me.*

Naomi nodded. "Just two minutes."

Bennett tore his gaze from Augie long enough to see her drifting off to sleep. Within a few seconds, her soft breathing suggested she'd fallen asleep. He whispered to the baby, "You have the most beautiful mommy."

Augie never released his hold on Bennett's finger, and his stare fixed on him as though asking his intentions. In that moment, Bennett promised his commitment to Naomi and Augie. Even if she rejected him romantically, he'd be there for them and help any way possible. If Naomi allowed him. Because the idea of being away from either of them was unbearable.

The night passed quickly. Naomi had gotten short bouts of sleep between Augie's grunts. It might take a while for them both to get their schedules lined up. Morning sunlight streamed through the blinds, and gratitude filled her heart. In juxtaposition, the new day reminded her that today she'd part ways with Bennett. She glanced around the room.

True to his word, Bennett hadn't left her side, except a few minutes ago, upon her request for a blueberry scone.

Their time was ending, and she needed to accept that. She'd contemplated telling him a hundred different ways that she'd fallen in love with him. But he'd chalk it up to the emotions arising from Jones's attack and Augie's delivery. As Selena had said, he'd see it as emotional attachment during trauma. She'd treasure their moments—even if it was filled with life-threatening events—and hope they maintained a friendship.

Naomi thanked God for the time they'd had, and she prayed Bennett would find love again—with or without her.

Augie sighed, regaining her attention. He slept, soft breaths emitting from his perfect rosebud mouth.

Naomi brushed her lips over his head, inhaling his sweet scent that filled her heart with the purest contentment. She glanced at her cell phone on the bed table. Still nothing from Evan. She'd sent a picture of Augie along with his birth information. But knowing her brother, he got busy at work and couldn't leave as planned. He'd show up. She considered sending a follow-up message, but didn't want to annoy him. Evan was a faithful brother. He'd never let her down.

The door opened, and Bennett entered, carrying a paper sack. "You wouldn't believe the line for that coffee cart downstairs."

"Thank you for enduring it," Naomi said, pushing herself to a sitting position.

Bennett set the scone on the bed table and added a few napkins. "How about if I hold Augie while you eat."

"You talked me into it." She gently passed her son to Bennett, wrapped tightly like a burrito in his blanket.

"Sleeping good?"

"Now—" she snorted "—if he could figure that out between two and four a.m., that would be great."

Bennett lowered himself into the chair beside her bed. "Any word from Evan?"

"No, but he'll be here," she assured him and herself. Naomi extracted the scone from the paper covering and broke off a section. It melted in her mouth. "Best. Scone. Ever."

Bennett chuckled. "I aim to please." His brown eyes captured hers. There was a new tenderness she'd not seen before.

"Why are you looking at me like that?" Warmth radiated up Naomi's neck. She munched on her breakfast, stalling for time.

Augie stirred and Bennett glanced down, then jerked to look at Naomi. "Is something wrong?" His eyebrows peaked. "Should I get the doctor?"

Naomi chuckled. "He's fine," she assured between bites of the scone. "He's just dreaming."

Bennett exhaled. "Whew. Okay." His shoulders visibly relaxed.

She relished the sight of Augie cradled against Bennett's muscled chest, outlined beneath the light T-shirt he wore. "I need help, little man," he whispered to the baby.

Naomi tilted her head, hanging on his every word.

"See, I wanna talk to your mommy, but I could use some advice on the best way to do that." Bennett lifted Augie closer to his ear as though listening.

A grin tugged at Naomi's lips at the silliness.

"Roger that. Okay. Thanks."

Augie grunted, then emitted a tiny mewing, his face screwed up in protest.

"I guess he's missing you already," Bennett chuckled.

Naomi took one more bite of the scone, then set it on the bed tray. "The feeling is mutual."

Bennett gently passed the infant to Naomi.

"What's up, Augie?" At the sound of her voice, Augie calmed, his wide eyes watching her. She nestled him, memorizing every detail of her son. "And what great wisdom did Augie offer you?"

He leaned closer, putting his hands flat on his thighs. "Naomi, I have to tell you something."

She swallowed hard, bracing her heart for his goodbye speech, and plastered on a smile. "It's all right, Bennett. You don't have to say anything. I've enjoyed our time together and would be grateful if we stayed friends. If you want to."

"I've fallen in love with you."

Had she heard him correctly?

He'd paused, eyes fixed on hers. Anticipation in his expression.

"You what?"

"Not the reaction I was going for, but it's not a rejection, right?" He smiled and her heart melted straight to the floor.

"With me?" *Brilliant, Naomi.* Why had she said that? "But you said…"

"Let's just say I had an epiphany yesterday about trust and faith. I've put them both in the wrong things and people. God alone deserves them." His brown eyes bore into hers.

"I'd agree with that."

"I recognize it's poor timing. You have your hands full. But I couldn't wait another second." He glanced down. "I needed to tell you I've fallen in love with you. And the funny thing is, I want to trust again. To love again. Seeing you and Augie makes me want to be a part of this something wonderful you two have going on."

Naomi studied Augie. Was Bennett certain what he was getting into? She couldn't afford to make a mistake by casually dating. "We come as a packaged deal. A ready-made family." She offered him the out he needed.

"Yep, like getting the best of both worlds. I've wasted too much time running away from love and a future with kids and a wife. I never realized I wanted that until you came into my life."

She blinked. "Bennett, I'm a little foggy here between lack

of sleep and people trying to kill me. Just to make sure I'm understanding you correctly… What're you saying?"

"Naomi, I want to marry you, be a father to Augie, and have a future with you both. The whole family deal."

"A few days ago, you were determined to arrest me as a serial killer." Her tone was teasing, and she was grateful Bennett didn't appear offended.

"Well, that's what brought us together in proximity. But your incredible faith and compassion and beauty and humor—those are the things that stole my heart, Naomi."

"You won't arrest me for robbery?"

Bennett laughed. "Nope, but I'd take fifty to life with you."

"Then I'll admit to being guilty as charged." Naomi's heart swelled until she thought it would burst. "Bennett, I am so glad to hear you say that. I'm madly in love with you."

"Sorry it took me so long to get here."

"You were worth the wait."

He leaned closer. "Does that mean you'll allow me to court you—for a short time—and marry you super soon?"

"Yes."

Bennett got to his feet, standing beside her. "I'd like to kiss you now."

"Don't let me hold you back. Besides, my arms are full." She gestured toward Augie, contentedly snoozing.

"A captive audience. I love it."

Naomi lifted her chin, and Bennett pressed his lips against hers. Once they connected, the hunger grew stronger, bringing to life all the hopes and dreams for their future.

"Ahem." A woman's voice interrupted with the sound of her clearing her throat.

Regretfully, Naomi and Bennett parted but kept their heads close together as they both turned to see Selena standing in the door holding a giant stuffed giraffe. "Didn't mean to interrupt."

"No. It's okay. We've got a lifetime to figure it out," Bennett said with a wink. "Come on in. I need to grab a bottle of water. Be right back." He excused himself from the room, and Naomi immediately missed him.

"Didn't expect to see that," Selena said, approaching with the stuffed animal.

An awkward silence hovered between them. Would Selena disapprove?

"It's about time."

Wait. What? Naomi's neck jerked upright, and her gaze landed on Selena.

"The attraction was pitifully obvious." She gently placed the giraffe at the foot of Naomi's bed, then dropped onto the chair beside her. "When's the wedding?"

"Soon, by the way Bennett spoke."

"I'm dumbfounded."

Her heart deflated at the presumed disapproval.

A genuine smile covered Selena's face. "Oh, Naomi. No, it's great!"

"Really?" Naomi exhaled relief.

"Absolutely. Bennett's a sound judge of character, and you're as real as they come. It's a wonderful thing." Selena inched closer. "Is there any possibility that I could hold your precious baby?"

She turned and spotted the sink in the corner of the room. Selena quickly hurried to it, not waiting for Naomi's response. She washed her hands and returned. "Okay, let me try that again. Now, could I possibly hold your beautiful baby?"

"Absolutely." Naomi adjusted Augie and passed him to Selena. "Meet August Lee."

A soft gasp escaped her lips as she glanced down at Naomi's son. "Oh, he's perfect."

"I agree, but I'm horribly biased."

"Makes me optimistic that I'll find love again."

"I thought you'd given up on romance."

"I had, but remember that ex I told you about?" Selena leaned to the side, exposing a vulnerability in her green irises.

"Yeah," Naomi urged conspiratorially.

"Turns out they just granted him a court hearing for new evidence they found that might prove he's not guilty."

"Wow, that's huge. What do you think of it all?"

Selena shrugged. "I don't know."

"But…"

"True confessions?" She glanced up, meeting Naomi's eyes. "Am I dreaming to hope it's true?"

"Never. I like inconceivable situations that become possible." Naomi smiled. "Bennett and I are proof it happens. I'll have to explain to Augie that we fell in love while Bennett was preparing to charge and arrest me as the Rocky Mountain Killer."

"From serial killer to bride." Selena laughed. "Sounds like a reality TV show."

"I should probably wait until Augie is thirty-five to share that."

The women fell into a burst of giggles.

Bennett returned, and Selena faced him, still cradling Augie. "Congratulations!" Her cell phone rang, and she frowned. "Ah, I don't want to give him up."

"You aren't limited to one holding," Naomi promised.

"Okay." Selena reluctantly passed Augie to Bennett. "I'll be right back. It's Chase. Can I tell the team the good news?"

"Yes!" Bennett moved closer to Naomi.

Selena hurried from the room, leaving them alone.

"I love you, Naomi."

"I love you, Bennett."

"Are you going to keep Carr-Cavanagh as your name?"

"That might be a little much with Ford, too." She tilted her head. "Actually, it's the prime opportunity for a fresh start. Naomi Ford."

He kissed her forehead. "I like the sound of that."

"Me too." And in that moment, Naomi realized everything she'd ever wanted was real, present and in her life. "Lord, thank you. You really go above and beyond with blessings."

"Amen," Bennett said, capturing her lips again in a kiss.

* * * * *

If you enjoyed this story, don't miss
Chasing Justice
the next book in the Mountain Country K-9 Unit series!

Baby Protection Mission
by Laura Scott, April 2024

Her Duty Bound Defender
by Sharee Stover, May 2024

Chasing Justice
by Valerie Hansen, June 2024

Crime Scene Secrets
by Maggie K. Black, July 2024

Montana Abduction Rescue
by Jodie Bailey, August 2024

Trail of Threats
by Jessica R. Patch, September 2024

Tracing a Killer
by Sharon Dunn, October 2024

Search and Detect
by Terri Reed, November 2024

Christmas K-9 Guardians
by Lenora Worth and Katy Lee, December 2024

Available only from Love Inspired Suspense.
Discover more at LoveInspired.com.

Dear Reader,

Thank you for joining Naomi, Bennett, and K-9 Spike on their wild adventure. Colorado is my home state, so I loved returning there with them.

Although I've never personally owned a beagle like Spike, I've had close friends who did. I could hear Spike's distinguishable beagle bark every time I wrote a scene with him. What fun!

I love hearing from readers, so let's stay in touch! Please join my newsletter, where you'll be the first to hear about my new releases and get behind the scenes exclusives on my books. Sign up or contact me at my website: www.shareestover.com.

Blessings to you,
Sharee